Amazon #10 5/19

SDC
GOULD
DEAD
3

Gould, JJ

JUL 2 4 2019

Dead End
Dead Air ; 3

DISCARDED
Huron Public Library

A novel by J. J. Gould

© J. J. Gould
Published 2018

ISBN-13: 978-1984392329

ISBN-10: 1984392328

HURON PUBLIC LIBRARY
521 DAKOTA AVE S
HURON, SD 57350-2797

Dedication:

To Bill Hoff: Thanks for the Sumatran Blend.

Acknowledgements

Writing a book can be challenging. Printing, formatting and publishing is far, far worse. Thank you, Rollan Wengert, for doing the worst part.

Prologue

Schmidt

Herr Pfarrer Schmidt's steps echoed down the north aisle of the empty cathedral. To his right, the pew-filled nave was cast in dark shadows. There was a loud pounding at the heavy oak doors outside the north transept. Normally, such commotion this time of the night would have been a cause for concern, but this was the second night, and the portly priest was ready for them.

In for a penny.

Schmidt's mind strayed to the saying that seemed to have been part of his existence ever since the Nazis took over and the trouble began. It had been a favorite of the bishop's, spoken from the pulpit in an effort to encourage the parishioners to stand up to the brown shirts and the anti-Catholic rhetoric the radical Nazi party was spewing out. "If we are in for a penny, we must be in for a pound," he would say.

As a newly frocked priest, Schmidt had flinched at the phrase, first because it would be sure to inflame the thugs who wore the brown shirts, bullies to a man. They were spoiling for precious things to smash, buildings to loot, innocents to drag out and beat up in the middle of the night. Second, it was an English saying, not a German one, and was sure to be reported to those in the party.

That had been in the early days, before the purging of the Catholic Church, the capitulation of the Pope with the toothless Reichskonkordat, the fear of the godless communists, and the Night of the Long Knives. Now the courageous bishop was gone, and many of the more outspoken priests as well—all arrested in the middle of the night and probably dead.

In the early days, Schmidt had not made a firm decision and did not know what to think about the new party or what exactly his faith and his church should do about it. Twelve years into this miserable Third Reich, he was serving as de facto bishop, clinging to safety, trying to do his job as a shepherd of God's flock, trying to find the right place to turn, and trying to make black-and-white decisions in a world that only seemed to offer gray ones.

Click, click, click. His hurried steps passed the enormous dome that soared up over the center of the church, separating the masses from the choir and altar, its majesty lost in the gloom of the night and the pressure of the coming meeting.

Again, the pounding.

"Yes, yes, I am coming." He said it more to himself than to whoever was knocking.

The centuries-old cathedral was laid out like an enormous cross. The main part was the nave, where the congregation and choir sat and where the altar was located. Crossing it on either side of the dome were the two smaller altars and seating areas. The one on the south featured the statue of Saint Mary, frequented by the devout wives and mothers of the flock. On the north was the altar to Saint Joseph, which served the admittedly smaller number of male parishioners, many of whom were scared, broken soldiers with burdens to confess.

The insistent pounding was coming from the exterior door on the north transept to the chapel of Saint Joseph. Schmidt unlatched the massive oak double doors and swung them out with ponderous dignity on wrought iron hinges.

The three men outside pushed their way in—no greeting, no reverence.

Swine.

Obersturmführer Klein looked down at Schmidt from his greasy bulk. The smell of his sweat added a sharp tang to the faint musty smell of the cathedral's interior.

"You are late, Herr Pfarrer Schmidt. We agreed that you would be ready by one thirty. And now you have increased the possibility of discovery." The voice tried to be angry and officious, but fear made it sound more like a whining complaint.

Schmidt bowed his head slightly, a vague gesture that could have meant subservience, politeness, or even contempt. "There is no need for concern, my sons. I am here alone. Let us continue through these doors to where we can discuss your wishes."

That was a bit of gamesmanship. By meeting them within sight of the altar and by calling them sons, Schmidt hoped to gain some authority. His plan somewhat worked. Klein's officious, contemptuous stance dropped a note or two, and he appeared almost civil as Schmidt closed the doors and escorted them below the high altar to a small office where the frocks, candles, and various other religious items were stored.

The three stood while Schmidt sat on an intricately carved chair that had been removed from behind the pulpit in the last remodeling decades earlier. Too holy to be thrown away, it served as a throne of sorts. Choosing it as his seat was another bit of gamesmanship on Schmidt's part.

Obersturmführer Klein, once settled in the room, tried to assume his authority again. He removed his brown wool overcoat—the late winter still had its bite—and draped it over the head of a nearby statue of Saint Mary, which, like the chair, was being stored in the room. He perched his peaked officer's cap on top of that. The move was a bit of insolence, his part of the chess match. "You have checked with your superiors," Obersturmführer Klein said. It was not a question.

"It is possible, although not with precedence," Schmidt said.

The third man, dressed in the menacing black of an SS Hauptsturmführer, leaned forward. "You sniveling coward. You cower in your sheep's costume and ridiculous superstitions, betraying everything the fatherland stands for. If it were in my power, I would shoot you now, and I may still do that."

The threat was real, and Schmidt knew it. This one was the most dangerous and had to be handled carefully.

In for a penny.

"Please understand, Herr Hauptsturmführer." Schmidt tried for a sense of calm and control that he did not feel. "With the political structure evolving"—he avoided the word collapsing—"and with enemy armies all around, transportation of bodies to consecrated grounds is not as simple as it once was."

"As we have said before, you simpleton, your position here exists only because it pleases the Führer." The SS officer's eyes shone with malice. "You have only to arrange the transportation of four caskets of American Catholic soldiers home for burial through the request of their families. This will not be done until after the... current conflict has died down and we have a chance to regroup."

The man was obviously delusional. The Führer he spoke of had not been heard from in weeks and was rumored to be hiding in a secret location, while American and Soviet armies rumbled toward Berlin. But as delusional as his fantasies might have been, the Luger in his holster was quite real, and Schmidt had no doubt of the man's willingness to use it.

Schmidt sighed. It would be a shame to die this close to the end of the war. "Well, Willi, shall we help these gentlemen?"

Willi was a shuffling hulk of a man of enormous strength with an untroubled and simple face. He was the village idiot and had sailed through the war unscathed and serene. But even he had been swept up in the last-ditch effort to save the fatherland. A cheap black-and-gray armband had been sewn to his patched coat. He was part of the Volkssturm, the "people's storm," a patriotic band of very old or very young men who would throw back the invading tanks with rocks, patriotism, and cheap armbands. Willi patted the armband and smiled at Schmidt proudly.

At the first meeting two days earlier, Schmidt had only met with Klein. The addition of two others, especially Willi, made things more complicated, if not impossible.

In for a penny.

He walked them back the way they'd come and opened the doors again to where the military two-and-a-half-ton truck was backed up and waiting, four army-green caskets in the back with names stenciled on the lids. Rumor had it that the Americans were at least two or three months away. Yet the bodies of four American soldiers were already prepared for their final trip home. First, they would be shipped to Italy, then Spain, then finally to a diocese in the American west that Schmidt had never heard of. The questions were obvious, but Schmidt knew that asking any of them would be life threatening.

And what they wanted to do was most irregular, bordering on sacrilegious. Normally, eight pallbearers would solemnly walk the casket up the broad stone steps, through the doors of Saint Joseph, and to the front of the church, but that night, Willi did most of the work. The caskets were bulky and heavy, over three hundred fifty pounds, yet Willi handled them with relative ease, sliding them off the truck and onto the handcart with a grunt and then pulling them up the broad, shallow stone stairs, the wheels of the cart jolting up the steps toward the bier. The cart's steel wheels on the polished stone steps echoed loudly through the cathedral.

Schmidt crossed himself. Such an invasion. Klein and the SS officer offered little help—they held the door and admonished him to be careful—careful!—as he pushed each casket off the cart and onto the bier, one at a time.

Cathedrals throughout Europe were not only places of worship but also places of burial. The walls and floors contained holy martyrs as well as rich and powerful leaders of the church. For dignified entombment, caskets were lowered slowly through the floor underneath the central dome of the cathedral on a platform that resembled an oversized dumbwaiter.

That was where Schmidt had laid the caskets. Once they were properly positioned on the lowering device, he pulled the lever, and the caskets slowly disappeared into the floor, one at a time, accompanied by a stately whirring of gears and cogs. Then the men processed down below to the basement and catacombs beneath the church, where the remains of countless saints of the church sat moldering in their individual tombs, a solemn gathering of silent witnesses.

Four times, a casket was placed on the bier. Four times, the lowering device whirred and clicked as the casket sank slowly through the floor. Four times, Schmidt pushed the heavy casket onto a waiting shelf as dust motes swirled through the dim shafts of light, the smell of mold, decay, and incense somber and powerful.

With each casket, Schmidt's hunches became more certain. Rumors and stories combined with his own intuition until everything clicked into place with the same whirring precision as the lowering device.

A priest naturally heard things. Schmidt had intercepted countless confessions meant to be sent to God's ears alone. When they were added together like pieces in a puzzle, an image gradually took form.

First, there were the disturbed confessions of troubled Catholic soldiers trying to absolve themselves of the sin of plundering the many rich Jewish merchants who lived in and around Thuringen. There were far more such stories than one might expect. The problem seemed bigger, more organized than individual greed could account for.

Then there was a worried widow, very devout, whose husband had worked in the salt mine in nearby Merkers. She tried to visit his grave just outside the mine entrance and was not allowed to. Whole sections had been cordoned off. Soldiers demanded to see her papers and threatened her with arrest.

"Herr Pfarrer, what would they want with an old salt mine?" she asked him.

And now there was the sudden disappearance of highly placed Nazi officials. No arrests, no announcements—they were just suddenly gone. The disappearances mysteriously coincided with movements of people within parts of the church known to sympathize with the Nazi cause. A far-off diocese in South America was suddenly awash with missionary zeal as men were sent to convert the Argentine masses.

The triumphant look on the SS officer's face sealed it.

He doesn't think it's over.

The four men were gathered around the caskets. In the gloom of the basement, dread, decay, tension, and triumph descended upon the two Nazi officers, cloaking them with an evil that was almost palpable. Squaring off against Schmidt, the two seemed to grow larger and more ominous. Feeling their threat, Schmidt backed away from them until he bumped against the heavy shelf containing the caskets.

"Thank you for your service, Herr Pfarrer. We will not be needing it anymore."

"You might as well tell me." Schmidt decided to tell them about his hunch. "If I wanted to hide something, something… precious, and I needed to find it someday—which might be months, or years or decades away—where in in the world could I hide it where I could be sure to locate it quickly and be sure that the random nature of man's progress wouldn't accidentally dig it up or destroy its landmarks? Where could I be certain it would lie undisturbed until I could retrieve it again with little or no chance of being seen?"

Schmidt, Klein, and the SS officer moved suddenly, each with different intent. The two Nazis grabbed for their sidearms, which were buckled in their holsters high up and on the side. They had nothing to fear from the lowly priest except his escape.

Schmidt's intent was more direct. He reached under a cobwebbed shelf and grabbed the double-barreled shotgun he had placed there earlier in the day—the same gun he had used as a boy to hunt geese and partridges with his grandfather. It had been a long time ago, but as with riding a bicycle, one never lost the knack.

He clicked the safety loose and leveled a shot directly into the SS officer, who was the biggest threat. He never had learned the man's name. Schmidt caught him full in the midsection. There was a huge blast of sound as the blood splattered out, a shower of black in the dimly lit tomb.

Ears ringing, Schmidt clicked loose the second safety and swung the gun to face a shocked, white-faced Klein, whose hands were raised in surrender, circling in front of the caskets, separating himself from his dead comrade.

After another blast, a little to the left, a large semicircle of Klein's left torso disappeared in a mist of blood and smoke. Slumping to the floor, Klein screamed once, twice. Schmidt's attention was not on him but on the shattered side of one of the caskets where, in the dim light, shone a small stack of what looked like gold bars.

I was right.

Willi was slumped in another corner, whimpering, his hands covering his ears. "Ow, ow, ow…"

The priest walked over to the casket and reached in, touching one of the bars. With reverence, he lifted it— heavy!—and held it out to the light. It was gold, all right, about eleven kilos, eight of them neatly placed and affixed in the center of the casket for balance, the approximate weight of a human body.

The heavy bar's luster was evident even in the poor light, the circle stamp with the swastika in the middle proof of its origin.

"Oww, oww, oww."

"There, there, Willi. It will be all right."

The plan was a good one. The war would soon be over. Bodies of American heroes would be sent home by the thousands. These four in particular would be buried in... Schmidt looked closer at the label on the casket, which read, "Corpus Christi Church, Dansing, South Dakota, USA."

Schmidt shrugged. He had never heard of it. Once shipped, the caskets would be buried in holy and sanctified South Dakota church ground. The government would mark the graves, and anyone who cared to could find and visit the graves anytime they chose.

Schmidt put the bar back carefully and, breaking the gun open, levered in another shell.

Willi looked at him wide-eyed.

In for a penny.

A blast rang out loud again in the deserted cathedral.

*****

The war was over, but Schell decided there was nothing exciting or valorous about it. Theodore "Teddy" Schell was just a boy in 1941. He'd gotten in at the tail end and was in basic training when the bombs dropped on Japan.

Still, he was up for a two-year hitch and was prepared to go wherever Uncle Sam sent him, which turned out to be Fort Eustis, Virginia, then the Transportation Corps... and finally, South Dakota.

He sighed and looked at the flat landscape out the window of the deuce-and-a-half-troop transport. About twenty more miles, he figured.

"Where the hell is Dansing?" Raske had just woken up. He rubbed his face slowly with both hands, the scrubbing motion distorting his words.

"Up the road." Schell nodded through the grimy windshield.

Raske resettled himself, adjusting the collar of his fatigues up around his chin. Within seconds he was back asleep, oblivious to the jouncing motions of the truck. Raske was from Chicago, a cadaverous man with perpetual stubble, who could and did sleep for impossibly long periods of time.

Schell sighed again and went back to brooding. The glamorous, see-the-world military life turned out to be the Army Graves Registration Service—which meant hauling dead bodies from where they'd died overseas to wherever they were supposed to be buried stateside. This particular three-day trip had started at Fort Snelling and worked its way from Saint Paul to Mankato, then to Alexandria, Watertown, Aberdeen, and finally Dansing,

South Dakota, a town he'd never heard of before he got the order.

They had to drive forty miles an hour along Highway 77 from Watertown, then west on Rt. 16 out of Sioux Falls with stops along the way through towns like Mitchell and Chamberlain, then Murdo and Stamford, before they headed north on the graded road. The trip was slow going—the military truck was made for less-traveled roads full of ruts and bumps. Dust passed easily through the door and settled thick and brown on the dash, seat, and green fatigues that Schell and Raske wore.

But at least the end was near. Schell geared down and stopped in front of the Catholic church on the edge of town, a big old stone monolith that stuck up like a granite thumb—a little piece of Europe in the middle of an American nowhere.

"... can't figure out why they didn't put 'em on the Milwaukee line." Raske was suddenly awake and clapping the dust off his clothes, picking up the conversation as if they had been talking the whole way. "Let's go, farm boy."

Raske leapt out of the cab and onto the ground, taking charge. He had an annoying habit of assuming that because he was from Chicago, he was smarter in all subjects and wiser in all circumstances, even though Schell was a corporal and two years older.

A priest came out of the rectory, a questioning look on his face.

"Hey, Father." Raske spoke as if they were long and familiar acquaintances. "Got some bodies for you."

Schell winced at the brusque delivery. "Uh, Father, what we mean is that we are from the Army GRS— Graves Registration Service—and we have some fallen soldiers to be returned home." He shook the dust off the clipboard in his hand and knocked some more off his fatigues.

The priest was unruffled. "Yes, I heard you were coming with um, four soldiers, I believe?"

Raske barged in. "Yep. You wanna gather the families for a look?"

Schell gave the priest a long-suffering gaze and a slight shrug of apology.

The priest nodded with a tolerant expression on his face. "Well, that's a strange thing, actually." He spoke with a slight Irish lilt. "We don't have any relations to the deceased that we can locate."

Schell was nonplussed. That had never happened before. Usually, there was someone to sign the paperwork, some bereaved person to whom he was supposed to offer awkward words of condolence.

Even Raske was taken aback. "Weird."

Schell was contemplating his next move. The thought of driving back three days to Saint Paul and waiting for more orders made his head hurt.

The priest spoke up. "But I do have direction from the Church. Apparently, these men requested burial here. There is documentation." His forms were much less dusty and written on expensive parchment, but they were forms nonetheless.

Schell relaxed. Forms meant orders, and orders were good.

Unloading the dull-green wooden caskets took about half an hour. The priest got some help from a few parishioners, and the four boxes were deposited on sawhorses in the shed behind the church next to a cemetery. Brown grass was tufted in and around the markers.

Schell kicked at the dusty ground with a practiced air. Sure is dry. Could use about three, four inches right now. Like his dad had said, you could take the boy off the farm, but you couldn't take the farm out of the boy.

"So, uh, is that it?" Schell stretched a crick out of his back.

"Yes, and thank you." The priest walked them back to their truck.

Only a day later did Raske start laughing. The next afternoon after a nap, he started chuckling as if they had talked about it the whole trip. "Heiliger. Max Heiliger."

Schell looked at him.

Raske was laughing louder. "What kinda mother names her kid Max Heiliger?"

"Why, does that mean something?"

"What, with a name like Schell, you don't sprechen sie Deutsch?'"

Schell's fingers tightened on the wheel, and his jaw set as he waited for Raske to finish having his fun.

"Heiliger means saint. So she named her kid Max Saint?" He laughed again. "Talk about wishful thinking. And the other ones. Rex, Felix, and Aurum..."

"What do those mean?"

"Not sure, but I think Rex is king, Felix is lucky—not so lucky for those boys, huh?" He laughed again.

Schell said nothing, thinking about the four soldiers.
His chemistry teacher in high school had showed his
class the periodic table and the symbols for each
element. Gold was Au. The Latin word for gold was
aurum.

He shook his head. He would have brought it up, but
he didn't like the way Raske was making fun of the
family.

Poor lady. Four sons dead, all killed in Germany,
buried back home all with Latin names like Lucky,
Greatest, King, and Gold. Well, hopefully she could find
them now and have a measure of peace.

Poor lady.

The First Week

Chapter 1 - Stacey Waltraub

Stacey hated losing, but he was going to have to do it. For seventeen years, he had lived in Dansing. Most of that time, he had been in law enforcement. The last twelve of those, he'd been sheriff of Dansing County, but in ten days—by about ten in the evening on the first Tuesday of November—the good people of Dansing would have kicked him out of a job.

A part of him, deep down, couldn't really blame them. He'd gotten the position mostly by accident. Vangie's father had been the sheriff, and her intervention had first gotten Stacey a job working around the office as a flunky of sorts.

But Virg, her father, must have seen something in him. Day by day, he'd taught Stacey about the workings of the job and the people of Dansing—the mostly good ones and the ones who were good mostly because a sheriff kept his eyes open. Then Virg died, and Stacey took over the job, tried to do it the way Virg would have wanted it done. Then Vangie died too, leaving a wound inside that had never really healed, and all he'd had left was the job. He'd ground along, doing the best he could. Soon the job would be gone too.

He sighed and put the truck in gear with a few remaining campaign signs in the back, blue paint on white plywood. "Elect Waltraub—Sheriff" was what they'd said the first time he ran. It was Vangie's idea to paint a red "RE-" in front of the "Elect" when it came time to run again. Just one of the million little practical things she'd done that made life easier.

Stacey sighed. Evangeline Grace was her name, and he mourned for her still. Strange, perhaps, that he hadn't gotten mad at God when He took her.

Stacey had always figured Vangie was too good for him anyway. "You're like my own guardian angel," he would say when they lay in bed at night.

"Hush, Stace—people don't turn into angels or vice versa. Read your Bible, and see for yourself."

"You're like an angel to me," he'd whisper, breathing in the scent at the nape of her neck.

"Well, do angels do this?" She'd turn in his arms with a low, bubbling laugh and make him fall even deeper in love.

Lost in the memory, Stacey rumbled along the dusty gravel, taking a shortcut over to Line, the last township left on his trip. Half the town of Line was in Dansing County and the other half in Bullock County. The county line cut right across its main street.

With a grunt of fatigue, Stacey heaved himself out of the old Dodge Power Wagon pickup and reached into the back for his maul and the signs.

He was not surprised that he had been beaten to it. Up and down the street were a couple of dozen signs, the bright plastic kind that wouldn't last a week in the wind and the weather but wouldn't have to. With the money Darren had, he could make new signs every day.

Darren White was a nice kid with a perfect pedigree. He'd been a Dansing High School quarterback the only year the team made it to state. After graduation, he had gone into the military followed by the police academy, then he'd spent some time in the Sioux Falls police force, and now he wanted to be sheriff. His grandfather on his mother's side was a Methodist pastor in the biggest church in Dansing. His grandfather on his father's side owned the biggest ranch in the county and half the buildings in Dansing. "Win with White—for Sheriff." The plastic signs showed a grinning, confident, handsome kid and were bracketed with pieces of stiff wire you could stick in the ground.

Stacey's signs consisted of rebar welded crossways to three-foot fence posts, the plywood bracketed between and tied tight with baling wire. Standing next to one of Darren's signs, he pounded his own with a couple of one-handed swings of the twelve-pound maul. Then he stepped back to look at his weatherworn sign, faded and immovable, next to its plastic counterpart.

There it is.

The two candidates were as different as the signs. At first, Stacey was embarrassed to have his signs appear

HURON PUBLIC LIBRARY
521 DAKOTA AVE S
HURON, SD 57350-2797

next to Darren's, but he finally decided that it was what it was, and the signs pretty much explained the difference between the two. One was old, worn, and stubborn, the other new, clean, and… plastic.

Jealousy was at the heart of the problem, Stacey had to admit. He just was not good at talking to any group larger than—well, any group. Darren, on the other hand, had been campaigning for weeks, telling about his experiences in law enforcement in the big city, clucking over the stories of the murders that had happened in Dansing in the recent months.

Stacey could feel the tide sway against him. People he had known for years showed a veiled reserve, and in the corners of cafés and the back of gatherings, he could feel the looks and sense that people were saying, "Let's give the kid a chance."

Not that anyone could accuse Stacey of anything. The murders in early spring were part of the April Fool's Day blizzard and had been a sort of badge of honor for the forgotten prairie town. And the tornado that swept through around the time of the Sturgis Rally, in August, was most definitely not his fault. But the death and disappearance of a number of townsfolk and several members of a biker gang had people wondering if a change might be a good idea. It was time to go with someone new, with different ideas of how to keep a town safe.

The late-October air had a little bite to it. Stacey tossed his maul in the back of the pickup and massaged a crick in his back, an old pulled muscle from back in the carny days. He chewed on his mustache, pondering. He was off duty, not in uniform.

Screw it. Clapping his cowboy hat down against the wind, Stacey headed for the County Line Bar and had a final drink to his occupation.

*****

When the Milwaukee Railroad had gone under, so had the rail spur that fed into Dansing. The rails were still there, so the elevator could lease a rail car to pick up the grain come harvest, but it was costly, so no one was really surprised when the elevator went bankrupt a few years later.

Stacey had been at the auction mostly out of curiosity and partly because there might be a need for law enforcement. There wasn't much to it, really—grain augers, office equipment, scales of all sizes and weights, and a 1953 Dodge Power Wagon originally used to haul feed and seed to area farmers. The business of supplying farmers had died down to unprofitability, and the jaunty red-with-black-fenders paint job had faded outdoors into a sunburned rust. All of the tires had gone flat, rotted out by the sun and weather, and casual inspection found places where a few generations of rats had used the upholstery for bedding.

"Does it run?" The answer was no. A run-down battery wouldn't crank it, and the gas had been left to rot in the tank.

"I bid fifty." The call came from an area scrapper looking for steel.

A look around the small circle of disinterested bidders made the auctioneer shrug. The auction was from a foreclosure run by a bank in Chicago, and if they didn't care, he didn't.

"One fifty." Stacey blurted out the bid, as surprised as everyone else. He had no interest and no real need for a beat-up truck.

The auctioneer needed no prodding. "Once-twice-sold!" he said and moved on to a pile of lumber sitting next in line.

Shaking his head at his folly, Stacey called Loren from the Amoco station to haul the truck in, and exactly one oil change, one battery, four tires, and one tank of gas later, he had a fully functioning faded truck.

"You want me to see about painting it, pulling the dents out?" Loren had a love for all things mechanical.

Stacey knew he would do good work. He'd studied the faded truck for a moment. The funeral had been a month earlier, and he still had a hard time thinking or making decisions.

He'd opened the door of the cab with a creak, studied its sun-faded interior, and sighed. "Nah."

Chapter 2 - Rick

Fortune has a bare ass.

Adolf Heinrich had learned that when he was in prison. As a kid fresh out of the Hutterite colonies, he learned a lot of things. He learned that his accent was a problem and his first name, Adolf, was a bigger problem. He learned that people were not to be trusted, and when they said they had a simple job for you to do and the money was easy, the job was not easy, and it was probably illegal and the only reason they invited you in on it was to take advantage of you and leave you holding the bag.

He also learned that he was tough. After countless times of being beaten up, he was able to take the beatings and give enough back to discourage attackers. He learned that he could completely get rid of his accent if he needed to assert himself, and he could bring it back as thick as ever if he needed to make people underestimate him. He learned that his wide, bland face and wide, bland body were easily forgotten and

overlooked and that many people said things in earshot
that they wouldn't have said if he hadn't been so bland
looking. He learned that people often mistook hard work
for honesty, and because hard work had been drilled into
him ever since he was a small child, people commonly
assumed he was honest.

And he learned that he'd gotten the shaft as a kid,
growing up on a forgotten religious colony in the middle
of nowhere, and that God might be real, but He didn't
smite people anymore. Adolf learned that in the current
realm of God, he could do whatever he could get away
with, that he wouldn't be bothered or even punished if
he was clever, and that if there was an opportunity, he'd
better grab it and not wait.

And he learned that Fortune had a bare ass.

MacLean had said that. Like a banty rooster, the
little Scot would fight anybody and would not stop
talking. By the time they met, Heinrich had learned to go
only by his last name and had gotten rid of his accent,
and because he didn't mind MacLean's constant
talking—he even liked it—they sat at the same table at
mealtime and walked the yard together at exercise time.

MacLean had read a lot and liked to quote poetry
and speeches and stuff. His words were bigger, and
when he talked about Fortune having a forelock and
shaved behind, Heinrich did not get it.

"Rick"—MacLean was the first to use the name that
Heinrich afterward took to calling himself—"it's like
this: Fortune is the once-in-a-rare-while grand
opportunity that walks right past you. You see her
coming and think, 'This could be it.' And while you're

thinking about it, she's coming right by you and picking up speed. And there is her forelock, a big hunk of hair, and just when you think, 'Hey, maybe I should grab on and see where she takes me,' she's gone past, and now when you think you'd like to grab on, you see it's too late—there is no more hair to grab onto. She is shaved behind."

"So Fortune is a girl, and she's got a bare ass?"

MacLean found that funny. "Yes, Rick. Commonly put, but clever and concise. If you find an angle or opportunity, you better act while you can, because Fortune, as you so accurately phrased it, has a bare ass."

Heinrich was definitely thinking of that when he happened to meet up with the senile old Kraut named Schmidt.

Chapter 3 - Stacey

The County Line was a questionable place to have a drink, but Stacey was tired and out of uniform, and besides all that, he would be out of work in a few short days, so what difference would it make anyway?

Once inside, Stacey saw things hadn't changed much. Eyes adjusting to the dark, he could see the dotted fluorescent stripe painted down the middle of the floor. On one side of the stripe was painted "Dansing," and on the other was painted "Bullock." It was more than a gimmick—the laws of the counties were different.

In Dansing County, the bars closed at two in the morning, one hour earlier than in Bullock County. Also, Bullock County allowed strippers, and during certain times of the year, Bob Schaumeit, the slightly shady owner of the bar, would hire some girls from Rapid City or elsewhere to make a couple of bucks.

Since it was still pheasant season and nearing dusk, the bar was surprisingly full, and Bob didn't recognize Stacey right away. "Hey, Sheriff, didn't see you there."

Then he added defensively, "I ain't doing nothing wrong— strippers are across the line, perfectly legal."

Stacey nodded wryly. It was doubtful that Bob Schaumeit was ever perfectly legal. He ran a mostly cash business, and the sheriff was fairly certain that little of it showed up on his tax returns.

He shrugged. Not my concern.

The beer out of the tap was tepid, without foam, and the change was all in two-dollar bills. Bob picked at a skin tag on his neck and tested the waters, nodding to the worn-out girl in the G-string who was standing on the platform, listlessly shuffling to the song on the jukebox. He waggled the bills in his hands meaningfully. "In case you wanna sit closer."

Bob's deal with the strippers was strictly commission, a fifty-fifty split of whatever they took. To increase the odds during stripper season, Bob did not make change with dollar bills, and for certain times of the year, as the cash worked its way through the local economy, the people of Dansing found themselves with an abundance of two-dollar bills and a vague impulse to wash their hands after handling them.

Stacey did not take the bait, so Bob tried a new tack. "So the election's coming up." It was a subtle dig. He'd had a few run-ins with Stacey over the years and would no doubt be delighted to see Stacey knocked down a couple of pegs.

Stacey did not respond but just took the money with a grunt and headed to the Dansing side of the bar, choosing a table away from the crowd.

And it was crowded, by Dansing standards. About thirty men, mostly hunters from out of state, were relaxing after a day in the fields, listening to country music on the jukebox, about a third of them leering at the stripper in a way that made Stacey ashamed for them.

He was deciding between playing a game of pool on the threadbare table in the corner or just going home to his lonely solitude when the disturbance started. He wasn't sure why the woman was there in the first place. She obviously was Not From Around Here, which made her outside of the protection of the town norms. In the second place, she was dressed all wrong for the time of year and especially for the bar—and that was probably why the trouble had started.

Four hunters were sitting between the door and the bar, loud talkers, big and brash. They probably belonged to the new SUV out front. Stacy had noticed it on the way in, a habit you pick up in law enforcement. The car's plates had a 1, which meant it was from Sioux Falls. In South Dakota, most of the counties were numbered according to the alphabet, and you could see a 16 on a plate and tell, for example, it was registered in Dansing County. For the top ten most populated counties, however, lawmakers had given up the alphabet and gone according to population.

Since Sioux Falls was the biggest city in the state, all the plates from that county began with the number 1. The numbering system was a sure way to find the strangers—and more than a few assholes—in town. These four were most probably from out of state, because their outfits were new and high end. Stacey

figured them for rich business types visiting Flyover
Land for a rare adventure in the empty west. They'd
probably landed at the Sioux Falls Airport and hired a
rental vehicle for the very long drive to the middle of
nowhere and the edge of his county.

The four were heckling the stripper, shouting insults,
and trying to outdo each other. Their camo pants and
boots were still on, but they had stripped off their jackets
and were wearing thermal undershirts. They were big
guys, could have been ex-football players, maybe gym
rats, drunk enough to start feeling their oats.

The woman's timing was terrible. When she walked
in, she stumbled a little in the dark, heels catching on the
rough floor, and fell into the table where the four
rowdies sat. She looked flustered and said something
that Stacey could not hear in all the noise. She was
dressed like a lawyer or executive—black skirt and
jacket, white blouse, pearls, the whole bit.

"Hey, this is what I'm talking about!" shouted the
largest hunter, a big guy with a red beard. "Go show us
your stuff!" He grabbed at the girl and shoved her
toward the stage. Her outfit was not a costume, but it
looked like it could have been one. The rest of the bar
started shouting and whistling.

She was confused and did not understand the
situation at first. When she saw the stripper, though, her
face immediately flushed. In anger, she turned to the
nearest hunter, planted her feet, and swung from her
hips. SLAP! The sharp crack of her hand on the side of
Red Beard's face rang out. Her eyes were furious.

"Oh, ho!" The song had ended on the jukebox, and shouts of approval from the rest of the hunters filled the void.

Red Beard was angry. "You little bitch." He grabbed her by the arms. He was easily twice her size.

Fighting with fury, the woman stomped down on his instep and butted his nose with her forehead. Lifting up quickly, she aimed a knee for his crotch, but he shifted and grabbed her again, this time from behind, pinning her elbows behind her.

The crowd was thrilled. Her face was flushed, and her suit was torn, her wild gaze showing the first signs of fear. And she was beautiful, dark skinned—Hawaiian maybe?—and full-figured, as if maybe she was a stripper and this was part of the show. And she was a stranger. What else could it be?

The cheers and jeers grew, the sound of thirty men away from civilization looking for a story to tell when they got home.

"Stop." Stacey's voice rang out with authority. He was still sitting alone in the corner. A crowd of mostly drunken men turned toward his voice.

"Fuck you, old timer." Red Beard was angry and aroused. He shoved the girl toward the dance floor.

"I. Said. Stop." Now Stacey was standing. He was not as tall as the red-bearded man but ready to challenge him anyway.

"You need a whuppin', Gramps?" Red dropped the struggling woman in favor of a new game.

"Get over here." Stacey gestured to the woman to stand behind him in the corner. Warily, the woman sidled across the twelve feet of bare floor that separated Stacey from the crowd.

Bob picked at his skin tag, obviously enjoying the moment. He would be of no help to Stacey.

The three other hunters stood up and rolled their shoulders loose, ready and eager.

Stacey gestured toward the striped line on the floor and smiled a tired smile at the red-bearded man. "You wanna come on over here and try?"

Chapter 4 - Ippy

She was in deep trouble, and she knew it right away.
How many times had her father warned her about paying
attention, avoiding trouble before it showed up? But the
mile-and-a-half walk after getting the flat tire, and the
blisters from those damn dress pumps, made her miss the
signs.

Her real name was Esmeralda Maria Johnson, and
she was a product of several cultures. Her grandfather on
her father's side was a Norwegian MP who'd married a
Korean while stationed in Seoul. Her grandfather on her
mother's side was a drill instructor of Haitian descent
who'd married a Cuban before the whole Castro blowup
happened.

Her dad was a master sergeant, and as a kid, she'd
moved from base to base, never more than a year or two
in the same place, so when asked about her lineage, she
usually replied, "I'm one hundred percent army."

A lifetime in and around army bases had taught her
how to take care of herself. Should have been smarter.

Slapping the jerk with the red beard was reflex, fighting against him was training, and struggling against the more powerful man was the edge of panic.

But as quickly as the trouble began, it evolved again to something very different but still dangerous. The noise was over, and a rather forlorn-looking cowboy with a droopy mustache was standing in front of her, shielding her from her adversaries, who were spread in a semicircle, thirty to one and edging in.

Trouble.

The men were drunk and dangerous. What they did or said could be forgotten or denied later. She had seen it happen before.

The cowboy seemed to know that too. "You." He pointed to the hunter with the red beard who had groped her. "You ain't from around here. We don't treat women that way." He motioned to a stripper in a G-string standing stock-still on a small platform. "And we shouldn't be treating them that way neither."

He grabbed a cue stick. "But the rules of that county are different than this one. In this one, I enforce the rules." With a quick flex of his wrists, he broke the cue stick in two, a gesture designed to intimidate the crowd.

It worked. There were murmurs among a few of them. That gray-haired cowboy is strong.

"Now, you fellas that came with this lawbreaker gotta make a decision and make it quick." Before they could react, the cowboy had stepped forward until he was about two feet from the man with the red beard. "You want any more trouble, junior?" He sniffed and spat on the floor.

Red Beard lunged at the shorter, older cowboy. That gave the cowboy the advantage. He was shorter, yes, but much thicker. While the hunter swung in with a short chop to the jaw, the cowboy simply stepped in hard, jabbing the blunt end of the cue stick directly into the solar plexus of the hunter, and dodged a blow that suddenly had no power behind it.

With a wheeze, the hunter sank to the floor. The cowboy ignored him and stared down the crowd. He pulled a pair of handcuffs out of his back pocket and dangled them. "Now, some of you don't know that I'm the sheriff of Dansing County." He pointed to the dotted line on the floor. "Since you don't, let me tell you a few things. I'm not interested in arresting folks who want to vacation out here. Nor do I want a bunch of paperwork that'll show up on your records when you get back home." He put the cuffs away. "All I ask is that you treat folks with respect and let bygones be bygones."

The cowboy picked the hunter up and set him on his feet. "Shake?" He held out his hand. Not out of fight yet, the red-haired man grabbed at the hand and squeezed, his forearms bulging. The cowboy did not seem surprised. With a shrug and a nod, he squeezed back— harder. Much harder.

Crack. The hunter's face turned white as the grip of the cowboy got tighter. Another crack.

The hunter wilted to the floor with a cry of pain. The cowboy let go of the hand, and the hunter held it carefully with his other hand as if it were a wounded bird.

The cowboy bent over the groaning man. "Sorry, mister. I don't have any hard feelings, but I bet that gal does. This probably makes her feel better."

With that, he headed toward the door and, opening it, motioned for her. "Ma'am?"

The door closed, and the world changed again. The dark, noise, and bar smell were gone, and just like that, it was another late afternoon on a mostly empty prairie. The late-fall breeze put a chill on Ippy's adrenaline and made her shiver.

"You okay?"

She nodded.

"Well, you better get out of here before something else happens. Where's your car?"

She motioned. "Back there. I got a flat."

He nodded again and opened the passenger door to his pickup. "All right, let's see."

Still wary from the recent close call, she got in and hugged the door of the rusty truck while he drove her out to the car. It was a Volkswagen Beetle. It had been cheap, and she was beginning to understand why. It sat with its hood open where she had left it.

The cowboy got out and looked. The right front tire was flat. A six-inch rip in the sun-checked sidewall made her wonder how bad the other tires were.

"There's no jack, or I'd have changed it myself." She wasn't helpless.

He looked at her. "No jack?"

She felt defensive. "I've only had the car a few weeks."

He nodded again and sighed. He pulled the spare out of the front hood then walked over and grabbed a tire iron out of the cab of his pickup and, in that same sort of world-weary way, stooped over and started loosening the bolts.

Once they were loose, he walked over again and grabbed a dusty spare tire out of the back of the pickup. His movements were slow and tired.

He walked the tire back to the Beetle and dumped it with a chump, creating a puff of dust on the gravel next to the front tire.

Why he was using his own spare tire was unclear. *It's not the same size.*

"I don't wanna mess your outfit up, but can you slide this tire under the axle in front? We'll need it to hold up the front end while we get your spare swapped out."

"Yeah, I can. No problem." Well, there was a problem. It was her only good outfit, and it would be a long time before she could afford to replace or mend it. Oh well.

Nodding absentmindedly, the cowboy walked to the front bumper, sighed, and settled down like a weightlifter. With a soft grunt, he lifted the front of the VW off the ground.

Holy shit! Amazed, she quickly scooted the tire into place, and he set the car back down with a grunt.

"Man, you are strong."

He shrugged, maybe a little embarrassed. "On a Beetle, all the weight's in the back."

Slow and sure, he put the spare on, tightened the bolts, and clapped on the hubcap with his hand, setting it in place with a few practiced whacks from the heel of his hand. That done, he walked around the front and, with the same grunt, lifted again while she scooted the truck tire out from underneath.

Once the car was on the ground again, he clapped his hands on his faded jeans, making them only slightly less dusty, and then nodded at her. "There you go."

"Thanks," she said lamely. She thought she should shake his hand, but he seemed a little dangerous, and his hands were still dirty, and how the hell was she going to clean her outfit as it was? The space of time drew out. "Uh, my name's Ippy."

He raised an eyebrow.

"It's a nickname. My dad was stationed in Panama when I was a kid, and when we moved on, they called me the Girl from Ipanema. You know, like the song."

He looked at her sadly and nodded. "That was my wife's favorite song." He nodded again and walked to his truck. The door opened with a slight squeal.

She called out, "So are you the sheriff?"

"For a few more days." He gave a slight shrug before he slammed the door and drove off.

****

Ippy had met her husband while in the army, and it was love and hate at first sight—she'd loved him, and her grandmother had hated him. Well, her grandmother had warned her not to be fooled by his beautiful eyes, his white teeth, or his charm. "He is a snake." Her Cuban accent was thick and got thicker when she was upset. But Ippy was young and married him anyway.

She stuck it out for eighteen years. They had no children, because he didn't want any. He had left the army because it was stifling him. They had no money saved, because he'd spent it. He had no work because of a nagging back injury or a racist boss or job that was beneath him.

And while he was home, supposedly looking for a job that wasn't beneath him, she found the two of them. He was above, the blond girl from the temp agency was beneath, and despite his bad back, both of them were straining away on a newly purchased mattress she had saved for months to buy.

Off on her own, pushing forty and starting over, she took her GI Bill money and spent it at Brown Institute, attending class with a bunch of squirrelly kids with dreams of major-market music stations. Her dreams had died of snakebite, and she had no lofty goals. Instead, she wanted a job right away and a chance to make a stable living.

Ike Kronforst was in charge of graduate placement. He looked a little like Hogan from Hogan's Heroes. "You want the best odds?"

"Yep."

He leaned back and steepled his fingers. "Fastest reliable money is news. I got a ton of stations looking for good radio reporters." He waved his hand toward a cluttered in-box. "They all want experience. You got great pipes, enough for a major market. I mean it. I send you some place to start out, you learn the ropes, give it a

good year, and call me back. I'll have the next place for
you then. Deal?"

"Deal." She stopped at the door and turned.
"Where's the station?"

He gave a smile that should have warned her. "Does
it matter?"

Chapter 5 - Rick

The nursing home in the suburbs of Philadelphia was called Sunny Haven, but it was neither. About as old as its average residents, Sunny Haven was dingy and rundown, with a depressing odor of urine and disinfectant that permeated the attitude of workers and residents alike.

Like most nursing homes, it didn't pay well and was chronically understaffed, which was probably the reason they hadn't bothered to check up on Rick's fake résumé. Convicted felons were seldom hired, so Rick had picked a fake last name and a fake Social Security number, figuring that by the time the IRS figured it out, he'd have moved on to the next opportunity. Rick did what he did best—worked hard, asked a lot of questions, earned some trust, and looked for things to steal.

The trouble was, there was nothing worth stealing. The nursing home was in a poor part of town, and the residents were poorer yet. Their possessions were mostly cheap crap furniture or dusty pictures of children and grandchildren who never came to visit. He had managed to make a copy of a key to the commissary, but stealing cases of food seemed like a last resort.

And then he met the old geezer in the lockdown wing. In its outdated brochures, Sunny Haven called the wing Safety Street to assure families that the demented loved ones they were dumping off would be safe and secure, but all the staff called it lockdown.

Lockdown was the place for old people who had lost their minds but not their motor skills. Its halls were populated with shuffling inhabitants looking for a way out—angry ones who demanded an answer to the same question they'd asked a minute earlier, perplexed ones who seemed baffled by everything and asked for help over and over, and deeply sad ones who cried and wailed the same lament from one minute to the next. All were completely ignored. Their words and curses and wails washed over the workers like moderately annoying noise.

When Fortune appeared that day, Rick was picking up bedpans. He got the shit work—the actual term staff members used—because he was new and didn't seem to mind. It gave him more unsupervised time to look around.

Then the priest showed up. "Yah, kann you tell me ver a Mr. Schmidt iss?"

Rick looked at him suspiciously for a moment. *Is he making fun of me?*

The rosy-cheeked, ginger-haired priest looked placidly back at him. He wore a heavy black-wool suit, black shoes and shirt, and white clerical collar.

"Sure, Father." Rick did not show his own accent, waiting to decide if it would help him or not.

As it happened, Mr. Schmidt was on his shit list, another term that they actually used at Sunny Haven. He remembered Schmidt's name because Rick had asked the wing supervisor to go down the list, carefully asking what each resident's particular issue was. The super had been impressed with his thoroughness, not knowing his real motive.

"So you are picking up the Schmidt shit!" The super laughed out loud at his tremendous wit.

Rick had pretended to be equally amused. Asshole.

Two doors down from where Rick and the priest were speaking was a double room. In one bed lay an obese, mostly catatonic man staring from his bed with empty eyes, a string of drool trailing down his unshaven cheek into a wide, wet pool on the bed sheet. The boyish priest with the German accent leaned over him, placed his hand on his matted hair, and murmured a blessing.

"Is that Schmidt?"

"No." The young man smiled. "Chust a man who needs some care." He reached for a Kleenex to dab away the drool. Rick checked out the stuff by the patient's bed: a baseball on a trophy stand and a few faded pictures, including one of a much younger version of the man in military dress, smiling.

After patting him gently on the head, the cherubic priest adjusted the blankets around the fat man as though tucking him into bed then turned his attention to the next patient. "Dis man here iss him." He pointed to the name at the head of the bed.

Schmidt was lying down in a reclining bed, arms restrained, moaning a loud, terrible moan. His face was gaunt and yellowed like an emaciated skeleton howling from his grave.

Yikes. Rick involuntarily backed away. "What's wrong with him?"

The young priest frowned. "He iss in deep pain."

"What for? He gets his meds—I see the nurse with the cart of medicine go down this hall twice a day."

"It iss not that kind of pain. His kind of pain no painkillers can reach."

The man named Schmidt must have heard them. Pulling against his restraints, he moaned a deep, horrible moan.

The priest leaned over the older man's bed. "Voss ist loss, mein kind?"

"Geld." The man moaned. "Reichsgeld."

Reichsgeld? Rick's ears perked up. Holy shit. The guy is German. Rick stepped to the side, listening to the conversation, which proceeded in German.

"My son, what is wrong?" the priest asked in German as Rick silently translated the words into English.

"Forgive me, Father, for I have sinned."

"How long since your last confession?"

The focus of the old man in bed changed, and his head turned a little as if talking to someone else in the room.

"Willi! I did it! I am so sorry!"

"Tell me about Willi."

"I was weak, Willi."

"What happened to Willi?" the priest asked.

"All that gold. I was a fool, Willi!"

The priest stepped closer. "What do you need to confess, my child?"

It seemed ridiculous for the cherubic-faced priest to call the cadaver in the bed a child. Rick was fascinated.

The old man looked suddenly cagey. His eyes narrowed, and his voice lowered as he confided to the priest by his bedside. "They never did find it, and so we can get it together. There for the taking."

"What is your sin, my child?"

Rick kept his face bland, hiding his frustration in his clenched fists. Screw that. What was that about gold?

Schmidt slumped back and away, groaning into a nether world of pain and guilt, moaning and mumbling.

"So what's that about?" Rick asked offhandedly.

The young priest shrugged. "He iss from Germany. I'm not sure why he is here, but I heard from a chaplain friend of mine that there vas a man who spoke German who was carrying a burden of guilt, so now I komm over to dis wing and include him in my rounds."

"So you speak German?"

"Yes, Pennsylvania Dutch." The priest looked proud of his heritage.

"So what's he say?"

The priest was evasive. "I am sorry. It iss a confession."

"Oh. Yeah. Sorry." Rick made himself look suitably abashed.

"Yes. Vell, it looks like I vill not be able to help him anymore today."

Schmidt was moaning, a deep, continuous moan. It gave Rick the creeps.

"You gonna come back?"

"Certainly. It iss the least I can do for another man of the cloth."

"You mean he's a priest too?"

The younger man nodded. "From Germany. So the chaplain told me. See." He pointed to a framed picture of a cathedral next to Schmidt's bedside with a string of rosary beads draped over it.

"Huh."

Rick showed the kid priest out and spent the rest of shit duty thinking about a German priest who kept talking about a lot of geld. Reichsgeld.

Nazi gold.

Old lady Fortune was near, and Rick sure as hell wasn't going to let her sneak past without grabbing on.

Chapter 6 - Father Patrick

Father Patrick's last day in Dansing surprised many people. An almost welcome part of the Dansing community, he had arrived one sunny summer morning forty years earlier, on his twenty-seventh birthday, and had worked diligently ever since, serving the needs of his flock. He was unfailingly polite and good-natured, kind to the elderly, and active with the youth. He visited the sick in the hospital and gave homilies that were no worse than the ones Father Michael gave.

Father Michael was referred to as "our old priest," and Father Patrick was referred to as "the new priest" because he'd replaced Father Michael. It didn't matter that Father Michael only served Dansing for four years before fleeing back home to Baltimore, or that Father Patrick was now gray haired and balding with two bad knees and about seventy-five extra pounds he had earned one bite at a time right there in Dansing. Even though he knew every name, and almost every secret, in town… he remained and would always remain the new priest.

This burden Father Patrick bore with good cheer and some resignation. He was also aware that he would remain almost welcome in the town as long as he lived. Through no fault of his own, Father Patrick had been born in Utica, New York, which made him Not From Around Here—another mark on his character that he bore with equal grace.

"Hello, Father Patrick."

"Hello, Doris. Beautiful day." Doris owned and ran the café in Dansing, the only real thriving business in town. Her tireless ability to serve vast plates of simple food in an efficient and cheap manner made her café a hub of caloric intake and gossip for the county, from its opening at five thirty in the morning until its closing at two in the afternoon.

Doris set a mug of coffee in front of him at his favorite table by the door. Father Patrick usually came in at nine in the morning and one in the afternoon to avoid the rush, and he ate with quiet relish whatever the daily special was. Monday was scalloped potatoes, Tuesday was roast beef, Wednesday was chicken potpie, Thursday was lasagna, Friday was fish fillet, and Saturday was whatever needed to be made to clean out the refrigerator. Dessert consisted of large servings featuring whatever fruit was in season. Sunday, Doris put her feet up for some well-deserved rest.

"I saved a piece of apple cobbler," Doris said in her usual gruff manner, as though trying to confess the favor and deny it at the same time.

Saving dessert was something Doris rarely did, but she made an exception for the priest because of a vague sense of kinship with him. She also was Not From Around Here—she'd married a Kneip boy, who brought her home from the army. She and the priest both loved food. She loved feeding it to hungry people with big appetites, and Father Patrick loved eating it. And a long time ago, she'd been baptized Catholic, a fact she'd shared with the priest once in a weak moment.

Father Patrick smiled as he looked out the window at the sun, which was becoming substantially weaker as it raced headlong toward winter.

"Yes, a beautiful day." Some found his habit of claiming every South Dakota day as beautiful a little annoying, but the priest was a man who found pleasure in simple things, and he really did find the seasons and bizarre weather patterns of the plains weirdly bewitching.

Many expected him to pray daily, but truth be told, much of the time the priest just gazed out his rectory window at the clouds, lost in thought.

It's kind of like praying.

The lasagna lay on the thick china plate, about the size of a patio block, cheese melting off the top. Leaning against the lasagna was a large piece of fresh-baked bread, toasted in the oven and dripping with garlic butter. As a nod to good nutrition, the special always came with a small helping of vegetables. That day, a dollop of canned corn sat in a little white dish with a sprig of green plucked from a series of mostly denuded parsley plants that hung by the south-facing window of the café.

Father Patrick didn't like parsley or wasting food. After a small internal struggle, he popped the sprig into his mouth. *It's good for you.*

Then, thinking of his mother, he ate the vegetables before tackling the main event with a clear conscience. *Mmm.*

Father Patrick ate with a slow reverence, chewing each bite thoroughly, setting his fork down between bites, and tasting each mouthful with his eyes closed. First, a bite of the lasagna. Chew, swallow. Then a nibble at the bread. Not too big a bite! It must last until the end of the lasagna.

Then he'd complete the cycle with a dab at his chin with a cloth napkin—Doris used white cotton napkins in her café. "A waste of my time, I can tell ya that." She always said it, and still each day, there they were.

Doris stood back a ways and watched. She was upfront about it. "I like to watch people eat my cooking." She especially seemed to like watching Father Patrick eat. "No disrespect, Padre. It's like watching the preparation of the sacraments."

The statement did nag at him a little bit. *I am guilty of gluttony.* The thought did not prevent him from looking forward to dessert, which arrived while he was eating the last bit of bread and lasagna—he had rationed both perfectly. Doris plopped it down with no ceremony. The dish spoke for itself—a big square of apple cobbler, the same size as the lasagna, steaming hot, with a large scoop of vanilla ice cream melting into a moat around its base. Doris had added a chuff of cinnamon on the top. A little color—very nice.

Father Patrick gauged his appetite. Still room! And with even more relish, he picked up his spoon and started in. Doris timed her desserts according to availability of the seasons. Apples were no longer cheap. The season was coming to an end, and this was the last apple cobbler she would make for the year. Next, there would be pumpkin desserts until Christmas.

He was about halfway through, a beatific smile on his face, when he stopped suddenly and looked at Doris. "Oh my."

He fell facedown into the unfinished cobbler, dead.

*****

No one said much at first out of respect for the dead. It took about a week for the first revisions:

"Well, he died happy, that's for sure."

"It's the way he would've wanted to go."

"He dug his grave with his teeth, enjoying every bite—not bad when you think about it."

Two months after his death came the second set of revisions:

"Hey, Doris, gimme a Father Patrick Special."

"Hey, Doris, serve me up a Last Supper."

Doris herself had a somewhat dark sense of humor, and because she really did believe Father Patrick had died happy, the Father Patrick Special became an actual menu item, something Father Michael could never claim and something Father Patrick himself would probably have taken a certain amount of pride in.

It took some deep thinking and about one full year after Father Patrick's sudden death before a rancher at the café sat back after coffee and said, "Y'know, when you think about it, all them murders and stuff around last November? It started right here when Father Patrick keeled over in his cobbler."

Chapter 7 - Geist

The name he was known by was Geist, although
throughout his career he'd had many names, and he
switched them like clothes to suit the mood, task, or
climate. His occupation took him many places, and for
that reason, he needed to speak many languages.

The circumstances of his youth made that easy for
him. His father was Russian, his mother Moroccan, and
both were Zionist Jews who'd moved to Israel while he
was still a baby. While growing up, he learned Hebrew
in school, both parents' languages at home, and Arabic
from the Palestinians who lived and worked in the
teeming capital city of Jerusalem.

From its earliest days, the tiny nation of Israel was in
peril. Surrounded and justifiably paranoid, the Israeli
security police force, the infamous Mossad, looked at all
Israeli students as possible soldiers in the never-ending
war against the enemies of the state.

And Geist was a particular standout, not just for his
ability to speak languages but also for his peculiar

aloofness. Slight of build and average in looks, he would sit with the back third of the class, doing work that was at the bottom third of the class. He had no real friends but didn't seem lonely. He had physical abilities but joined no sports teams or clubs.

His real gift, his truly spectacular ability, came when carefully placed Mossad agents, called talent scouts, casually brought up his name to teachers, neighbors, and coaches.

"Who?" they would ask. It seemed that he was invisible.

After a few gentle prompts and nudges, they would frown. "Hmm. Uh, he's okay…" There were no opinions, no stories, no anecdotes. He was a ghost.

Even when subtly approached and then more fully recruited, the boy himself seemed to have no real ambitions or dreams. He was suited to fading into the background of wherever he was.

As a recruit, the young man was gradually trained in all types of spy craft, hand-to-hand combat, and weapons. These he took in with the dreamy ease of a lackluster talent, never exciting comments, positive or negative, from his trainers.

Even as the legends of his exploits grew within the Mossad, there were those who were resistant to believing in his abilities.

"Who? Well, I guess I recall him, but I can't say that he ever struck me as someone with any real talent."

While others were given particularly difficult extractions or black operations involving helicopters and midnight drops and high-caliber weapons, he simply had one-man assignments. A certain person was a danger to the State of Israel. The Mossad would give the young man a name and show him a picture or two. The young man would nod vaguely at the information and then walk out the door and disappear.

Two months later, he would be back, and the person would be dead or missing, usually by way of some sort of accident or health incident. No investigations, no headlines—just an enemy of the state neutralized.

They took to calling him the Geist, the German word for ghost, a nickname that stuck and eventually became his code name, one that seemed to amuse him in a vague kind of way.

His career ended in the same murky way that it had begun. He was sent to Argentina to find an ex-Nazi. This one had ties to Nazi sympathizers in the German Catholic Church and was rumored to have access to ledgers and documents detailing where vast sums of stolen money were hidden away after the war. The money rightly belonged to millions of Jews, and the Nazi rightly deserved to be punished for his crimes.

Geist was trained in German and Portuguese and given a picture and a name. Then, with an unfocused nod, he walked out the door and disappeared. For good this time—he never returned, and he never reported in.

The rumored ex-Nazi disappeared too. The date of his disappearance was vague. There were no leads or suspects. It was as if they'd both vanished from the face of the earth.

Which was only half right.

Chapter 8 - Rick

After the Pennsylvania Dutch priest left, Rick found out
his name. Ansdorfer. He fished around a bit. No stories,
no gossip, so he had to be either a square shooter or new
to the job. Just a guy who wanted to help.

He found out that the Ansdorfer guy came around
twice a week. That gave Rick some time but not much.
Fortunately, workers were rarely seen in the wing
Schmidt was in, especially late at night, so Rick had time
to work on the problem.

He snuck into the room when no one was around and
spoke softly in German. "When was your last
confession, my child?"

"Ohhh, I'm sorry, Willi!"

"Confess your sin and be forgiven, my son."

Schmidt moaned. "No forgiveness for me, Willi.
What did I do? What did I do to you?"

Rick took a guess. "Did Willi take the gold from
you?"

Immediately, Schmidt drew back as if he'd been struck. His eyes became shrewd and distrustful. "Who are you?"

Rick repressed the urge to wring the old man's neck. He withdrew, keeping his voice calm and measured. "I will come back only once more. After then you must face the fires of hell alone with no chance for forgiveness."

He'd laid it on a little thick, maybe, but Schmidt didn't look so good. It would be so unfair to Rick if the scrawny old priest croaked before talking about the gold.

The next day was horrible. By the time Rick got to work, the visiting doctor had given the old geezer such a high dose of painkillers that the slavering old fool could utter nothing but moans and howls.

And the day after that was even worse. Schmidt's bed was empty, and a sterile cot, still wrapped in plastic, lay waiting for someone new. A cardboard box with the few possessions Schmidt still owned sat on the floor by the window.

"No!"

A bored nurse's aide overheard his cry as she walked by, pack of cigarettes in hand, heading for a smoke break. She gave him a sympathetic face, the kind put on for those who were suffering. "Yeah, too bad about the old priest. You knew him, huh?"

"Uh… yeah." Rick was suffering all right. *Scrawny piece of shit.*

"Yeah, he wouldn't stop yelling and moaning. Some kind of real pain. They took him over to the hospice wing about an hour ago."

"H-Hospice?"

"Yeah. They're gonna dose him with some serious morphine and see if that does the trick. Kill or cure, like they say."

"He's there now?"

"Yep. Poor old guy'll probably check out for good in the next day or so."

Rick nodded, deep in thought.

"Sorry, guy." The nurse clicked her tongue. "I didn't know he meant so much to you."

You have no idea.

Chapter 9 - Father Ansdorfer

Coincidence. Father Andrew Ansdorfer stared at the
typewritten index card on the cork bulletin board. Three
hours earlier, he had visited a nursing home and taken
the last confession of a German priest named Schmidt.
The man was crazed—delusional really.

Certainly the old priest had believed the story as he
relayed it, tears flowing down his cheeks, but the
random way his words crossed over decades, skipping
from detail to detail, made it hard to tell what was real
and what was hallucination. Yet three details kept
resurfacing over and over.

One was about some gold, Nazi gold. The second
was about murders. Who and how, Schmidt never said
clearly, but apparently, he had been involved in the
killing of at least one man named Willi. The third detail
involved the city of Danzig.

"What about Danzig?"

"It is there!"

"What do you wish to tell me about Danzig?"

The old man then shook his head back and forth, flecks of spittle at the corners of his mouth. "Nein! Amerika!"

"America?"

The man nodded and looked relieved, as though freed from his burden. "The church in Danzig."

"There's an American church in Danzig?"

The failing priest either did not hear the question or did not care about it anymore. His eyes were glazing over as he reached toward the small framed picture of the cathedral that sat near his bed in the hospice ward. Either accidentally or on purpose, he knocked it off the bedside, and it fell to the floor and broke.

Clicking his tongue, Father Ansdorfer reached down to pick up the pieces. It was not an ordinary frame, though. As he gathered up the bits of glass and wood, Ansdorfer could see that the frame had a false back—a secret compartment behind the frame—and there among the pieces was a small piece of... what?

"What is this?"

Even as he asked the question, he could see that Schmidt was dead, eyes focused to eternity, a small smile fixed and frozen on his face.

May God have mercy, my friend.

Ansdorfer closed the eyes of the dead man and said another prayer, folding Schmidt's hands across his chest as he did so. When he was finished, he looked again at the item in his hand. It was a gold nugget of some sort.

No, not a nugget. It looked like someone had taken a chisel and hammered a small wedge off of something larger. Heavy, though.

Ansdorfer hefted it in his hand, thinking about the old man's confession. Maybe not so crazy after all.

"Is he gone?"

The nursing-home orderly's questions made Ansdorfer jump, and without a thought, he plunged the piece of gold into his pocket.

"Thanks, Father. Thanks for coming over."

"It was nothing." Ansdorfer found himself shaking his head and backing away, feeling a nameless guilt.

Later, he made his way across town to the diocesan office in Philadelphia, an anonymous one-story structure that served the needs of the adjacent seminary and the far grander Cathedral Basilica of Saints Peter and Paul downtown. In the familiar musty gloom of the office, the priest stood at a waist-high counter, waiting to file paperwork into the row of stuffed steel cabinets looming in the background. Death, taxes, and paperwork: the curse of sinful man.

He dinged the little steel bell on the counter, in no particular hurry. Behind him was the Positions Needing Immediate Fulfillment board, a cluttered listing from all over the world. The board was a point of interest to the seminary students next door and a passing curiosity for Ansdorfer, who was looking for a place to serve closer to home.

He scanned the board, avoiding the old tattered listings—places far away from influence and opportunity—and searching for the freshly posted opportunities. And then he saw it:

Dansing.

Shocked, Ansdorfer stared at the ten-point font, his mouth dry.

Dansing, South Dakota: Corpus Christi parish, West Dakota diocese, has an immediate need for a young, energetic priest to serve this scenic plains community.

The phone number was listed.

On the counter, Ansdorfer found the well-thumbed index listing all of the parishes, churches, and priests and their office addresses and phone numbers. He checked under the letter D. The only thing remotely close to the name Danzig, which the crazed priest Schmidt had repeated over and over, was Dansing, South Dakota.

"Can I help you?"

The friendly question from the priestly clerk behind the desk almost made Ansdorfer jump out of his skin.

"No! I mean, yes, I'm just looking. Uh, Just looking for information about the posting for Corpus Christi Church in Dansing, South Dakota. And I have some chaplaincy paperwork to file. "

The priest took his paperwork and gave him a bemused look, "Are you sure it's"—he checked the index card—"Dansing you're looking for?"

Ansdorfer's hand was in his pocket, clasping the small piece of gold. "Yes. Yes, absolutely."

Chapter 10 - Darren White

Piece of cake.

Darren walked toward the KDAN studios, running a comb through his hair. It was not a TV station, of course, but appearances were important. He checked his image in the window of the real estate office as he walked by, a habit of his.

Nothing against ol' Walrus, but a guy's gotta start somewhere.

Grandpa White was right. It was time to settle down and get busy. He'd had his fun, but it was time to move forward. His grandfather had been the one to suggest running for sheriff.

"Son, it's time to start making a name for yourself, an' bein' sheriff is as good a way as any. Waltraub is slow an' a little stupid, especially when it comes to politics. With what happened this year, folks'll be lookin' for a fresh start. And that," he said, stroking his signature across a campaign donation check, "is you."

Darren had taken the check with little comment. Long ago, he and his parents had come to an understanding that Grandpa White had plans for his grandson and money was no object. And as usual, the crafty old rancher had a point. A cop himself, Darren had heard all about the murders that took place around the time of the April Fool's blizzard, first as station gossip, then on the national networks, and then in person when he came back to Dansing for Easter. It seemed the initial investigation into Marie Dormier's death had been a little loosey-goosey even for Dansing.

By May, he had moved back to Dansing and was living in a nice ranch house north of town, with a new pickup and a plan to be the next sheriff of Dansing County, all courtesy of his grandpa. That galled him a little bit, but his ambitions were bigger than Dansing and one pushy old man, so he accepted the man's help for the time being.

"Hey, Darren!" Larry Karl came out of the radio station, flagging him down. "Hey, hey! It's the man of the hour! Just in time. Say, I'm still doing my shift and only got a minute till I got to get back in and cue up another record. Would you be interested in doing some color at the football game this Friday? It's a home game, last of the season."

What Larry did not say was that Dansing's football team was pathetic, not having had a win in three years, and the season finale against Mobridge was going to be a bloodbath. Darren winced. Larry Karl was a blowhard with an exaggerated memory of his own high school sports prowess and an inflated opinion of his less-than-mediocre broadcasting ability.

The game would be interminably long, and no doubt, Larry would ask him to rehash the glory days when Darren was quarterback and the Dansing Prancers—the sad-but-true name of the team—made it to state, albeit eighth place, for nine-man football.

The offer probably wasn't fair, either, amounting to a glorified two-hour "Darren White for sheriff" commercial.

Karl seemed to sense his last thought. "You could talk about anything you want." His wink was obvious. Sheriff Waltraub had arrested Karl for driving his pickup into a ditch on a drunken Saturday night, and Karl had never forgiven the slight.

Darren nodded. Every vote counts. "Sure."

Karl clapped him on the back, hale and hearty. "Great! Get there about five thirty. I got some stories to tell, some of 'em not acceptable for broadcast if you know what I mean." He winked again.

Great. Darren followed him into the station. "Say, uh, Larry. I'm here 'cause of some sort of election forum? I got a call from a woman, don't remember her name."

Larry's expression worked through some blank looks before he raised an eyebrow and leered. "Oooohh."

Any further comment was cut short. The monitor in the outdated lobby was broadcasting silence, and Larry scooted through the studio door with surprising agility. Darren could see him through the grimy bay window of the lobby, grabbing a record with one hand and trailing a stream of yellow paper in the other. Once he was sprawling in a chair, he clicked on the microphone, bringing the monitor to life.

"The Big Neighbor, eight seventy, K-D-A-N. It is"—Larry glanced at a thermometer—"fifty-two degrees and a quarter to three in the p.m." Larry was using his radio voice, saying "BuHigg dNAY-burr" and "FuHIFTee Tyoo DuGreezz." Darren seldom listened to KDAN when Larry was on. His voice was like fingernails on a chalkboard.

While Larry was talking, Darren could see him scanning through the yellow ream of paper, stalling. "Soooo, let's taHAKE a look… at yahore farm markets…"

A small, mouselike woman who worked in the office came out, shaking her head. She rolled her eyes and turned down the monitor.

Thank you.

"Can I help you?"

She was too old for him, but he treated her to a smile anyway. *A vote's a vote.* "Yeah, I'm supposed to talk to someone at a forum of some kind?" He gave her a charming boyish shrug.

She simpered, "Oh, yes, Mr.—or should I say, Sheriff—White."

He gave an Aw, shucks smile. "Well, the election hasn't happened yet."

"Hey-hey!" Jack, the guy who ran the station, came bounding out of his office, out of breath from the fifteen-foot exertion. His real name was Jack Wilson, but he introduced himself as Happy Jack, which made him seem even more clownlike than he already was.

It was cool outside, but Jack's face was shiny, and a big half circle of sweat was looped under each armpit. "Thanks for stopping by, *Sheriff*." Jack winked and laughed helplessly, overcome with his own wit.

The smaller woman seemed annoyed and interrupted his rolling chuckle. "He wants to talk with the new girl."

"Ohh, yes!" Jack scrubbed his hands with delight. "But, Lois, I think you mean the *news* girl." That was followed by more uncontrolled mirth.

Darren and Lois gave him deadpan looks while he controlled himself.

"Anyway..." Jack stretched out the word into three long syllables while he retucked a loose shirt into his voluminous pants. "Her name is Esmeralda Johnson. She took over Stan Martin's job." He said the name Stan Martin like he was dropping the name of a celebrity— which he was, in a way. "She goes by her nickname Ippy, and she's definitely not a girl." The look he gave Lois out of the corner of his eye led Darren to believe Jack would fully like to explain the girl comment.

Just then a woman appeared from the back hallway. *Holy. Cow.*

"Are you Darren White?" The woman's expression was direct and open, her hair cut short like a boy's, though her skirt and suit jacket made her definitely not look like a boy.

She walked across the room and looked up at him. Closer up, Darren could see she was older than he'd thought at first, maybe even middle-aged. He gave her his best smile, the one that worked best with the ladies.

"I sure am. Glad to meetcha." He held her hand just a little too long. A little hint. "And your name is Izzy?"

"Ippy."

"Is that Hawaiian?" Darren usually liked college-aged girls, but he was rapidly reassessing his standards.

She looked at him coolly. "No."

Hot damn. Nothing like a challenge.

*****

Darren and the guys on the football team had hosted a kegger. Sheriff Walrus, as he was called by the players, had busted the party, flipped the flashers, and bango! It was everyone for themselves, easily running away from the older man with the bad knees and the drooping mustache.

Darren stopped chuckling to himself when he pulled into his driveway and saw Waltraub sitting on the porch of his folks' house. The house lights were off. The sheriff was there alone.

Uh-oh.

"No need to bother your folks just yet." The man's voice was quiet, and his form was cast in deep shadow. "Son, do you know about any field party out by Samuels? I thought I recognized some kids that might be friends of yours."

"No, sir." His smirk was long gone.

There was a pause in the dark.

"You sure?"

"Yessir." Darren was glad the poor light covered his flushed face.

"Well, I was afraid of that." The sheriff stood up and reached behind him. He pulled something from his jacket. It made a metallic clank when he tossed it onto a nearby chair. "Looks like some son of a gun stole the plate off your car while you wasn't lookin' and used it to incriminate you."

The sheriff leaned close, eyes solemn in the dim light. "Every kid needs some fun, but ever since I scraped Jess Bar off of the highway and had to go wake up his ma and tell her about her only child, I guess I've taken a harder line on parties. Trying to get a hold of the ringleaders, trying to stop another senseless death."

Now the sheriff was closer yet and very, very intimidating. "But I can see that that is not you. Good. I'm glad I don't have to write you up and ruin any prospects you might have for college, and I guess it's no harm now that you got your plate back."

He stepped off the porch, boards creaking quietly under his weight.

Then he'd turned back, face still shadowed under his hat. "But if that kid ever tries it again, he'll be in some serious trouble."

Chapter 11 - Ippy

As she led the kid in the white cowboy hat and shirt back
to the KDAN recording studio, Ippy was wondering for
the umpteenth time about her career choice. She was not
afraid of travel or new places—she liked them
actually—but the glamorous world of broadcast
journalism seemed a long way off.

"In here, please." She showed the kid into a room
paneled with dark wood and featuring a long Formica
conference table of the same dark hue. A large window
separated one wall from the KDAN studios. Larry Karl
was on the other side, leering at her through the murky
glass. This was the studio where occasional guests
would be featured, maybe a music combo or maybe a
group of 4-Hers. That day, Ippy chose to use the space to
record the kid running for sheriff. The way he was
looking at her made her want a large piece of furniture
between them and a window for observation.

The room already was set up for recording. Ippy
motioned for the kid, who looked vaguely familiar, to

take a seat. She strategically moved her tabletop microphone to keep him across that table and to avoid seeing Larry Karl.

She turned and punched the play and record buttons on the large reel-to-reel recorder then tapped the mic for volume and motioned for the kid to do the same. "Say something."

He leaned into the mic. "Hey there."

She sighed inwardly. *He must like cologne.*

"So to help me out, let me get the spelling of your name and pronunciation."

He leaned in again with an assured smile. "White, Darren White. D-A-R-R-E-N White, like the color."

"Okay, and your current address."

"Okay, but you're gonna have to help me out too."

"How so?"

"Well, tell me, what's a…"

So help me God, if he says "pretty little gal…"

"… young gal like you doing in Dansing?"

"Not so young anymore." Her expression was tight as she tried to keep her composure.

"You been a lot of places?" He sounded suggestive.

Ippy sighed. Might as well get it over with. "My dad was career military. I spent twenty in it myself before trying this out."

His eyebrow rose. "Twenty years?" He was quiet as he did the math then looked at her as if appraising a piece of livestock. "Wow. You're in good shape." Some of the suggestion came back into his tone. "Real good shape."

Ignoring the comment, she consulted her list. "I'm doing a quick interview with all the county and city candidates. Can you tell me which office you're running for?"

He smiled a little wider. "I'll be the next county sheriff."

Finally, it came to her why he was familiar. She had seen his face on campaign signs. "You're the one running for sheriff."

He smiled a little wider. "That's me. Time for a change."

She looked at him and compared him to the cowboy with the sad eyes and the dusty pickup. "What's wrong with the real sheriff?"

Chapter 12 - Rick

That bitch Fortune was not about to get by Rick this time. Hanging around the hospice wing, he bided his time, cleaning and listening, listening and cleaning. It didn't take long. A couple of nurses were drinking some bad coffee at the nurses' station, talking about the turnover, clicking their tongues.

"I mean, what the heck? I know it's depressing to see guys croakin' every day, but they're chaplains for God's sake! Now I gotta train a new guy, a good three hours outta my day, give him the keys..."

"Didja get the old set from the other guy?" There was a lot of concern about that. Missing and lost keys meant a whole shitload of memos.

"Yeah, yeah." She waved off the worry and returned to the story. "Anyway, I thought that maybe, maybe, this last guy might stick, y'know? The priest, I mean."

"The one with the accent? The Amish guy?"

"Not Amish—he's a Catholic, ya moron! That's why he's a priest."

The other nurse gave a cross look but no comeback—the story was more important than being insulted. Dutch, Amish, whatever.

"So you know that old priest guy that croaked?"

"The Kraut? The one that wailed alla time?"

"That's the one. So he's screaming, I mean, like, what the hell? And so this Father Squeamish guy runs over to catch him up. Y'know, the last rites—forgive me, Father, for I have sinned?"

"Yeah, yeah?"

"So, like, right away, the old guy calms down, and they start mumbling away in German, and bango! He's gone!"

"Who's gone?"

"They're both gone! The old guy, he's suddenly dead with, like, a smile on his face—y'know, Saint Peter and the pearly gates. And the other guy, he stumbles outta here like he's in some kinda trance. I ask him if he's okay, and he kinda jumps, y'know? Like I scared him or somethin'."

"Was he, like, freaked out?"

"Nah, not like that. I mean, I thought for sure he'd be back, but no—the super said he's gone, like, gone. Took off to work someplace else."

"Where?"

"How the hell should I know?"

*****

The priest at the diocesan office looked over the desk counter and lowered his voice. "I think he was g-a-y."

Rick knew that the secret of developing a connection was to mimic the movements of the other person. He leaned forward and lowered his voice. "Oh, really?"

The priest nodded. "It happens, you know. Priests get a frock, but they can't contain their urges. Then they get a little too close to some of the boys they work with and then flee as far as they can."

"And that's what happened." Rick gave a dismayed look.

"I bet. Why else would you take a position in Dakota?"

Rick said, "The state?" in an appalled tone.

"There's two of them." The priest nodded as he added that bit of trivia.

"I have a nephew who lives there! Should I warn the parents?"

The priest glanced at a piece of paper on his desk. "Does he live in Dansing, South Dakota?"

Chapter 13 - Father Ansdorfer

When Father Ansdorfer stepped off the bus, he looked around. Unbelievable. He had never been west of Pittsburgh his entire life, and there he was, in Dakota. South Dakota.

And it all happened so fast.

He had turned in his request, his paperwork had been processed—and then he'd gotten a long-distance call from Sioux Falls and a promise that regardless of how many applicants there were, the diocese would be patient and thorough and pray over all the applicants, trying to discern, with the help of the Holy Spirit, whom God was calling to serve the flock in Dansing, South Dakota.

Within two days, he received his formal charge to service in the mail. Must not have been many people for the Holy Spirit to decide between.

It would take three weeks for his belongings to be shipped. In the meantime, the bishop suggested that Father Ansdorfer fly out to South Dakota right away and get acclimated.

Ansdorfer hated flying and told the bishop he preferred to see the countryside unfold mile after mile instead of from forty thousand feet. The diocese didn't mind. It was certainly cheaper, so thirty butt-numbing hours later, Ansdorfer stepped off the bus and back about a hundred years.

No, that's not true. As the bus driver dumped Ansdorfer's two suitcases off the bottom bay of the Greyhound, the priest looked around and wondered what exactly made this feel like a different time.

Certainly they still had most of the stuff of civilization—electricity, cars, refrigerators, ribbons of flat roads stretching off in every direction.

It's the sounds.

A blast of wind pushed against Ansdorfer and made him clap his black fedora down tighter. The bus had chuffed and wheezed its way off and away to another possibly even more remote location, its diesel cloud whipped cleanly away, replaced by a fine blast of sand. As the bus faded away, its sound was replaced with...

Nothing.

No traffic, no construction, no jackhammers, stereos, sirens, air conditioners, hums, whirs, buzzes, or beeps. Just the wind. He wrapped his coat tightly around him. The sun was out but heading toward evening, and the wind had a bite.

He consulted his paperwork to confirm which hotel he was staying in. Edge O' Town. There it was, a two-story cinderblock building with faded paint and a tired look. Nothing fancy, but he didn't expect that. *I am here to serve.* The thought of his calling made his hand search for the piece of gold in his pocket.

If I find it, I will use it to serve the Church.

Grabbing the two suitcases, Ansdorfer struggled manfully against the wind and toward the motel. He set down one of the suitcases, and it immediately was pushed over by the wind. He leaned over, tipped it back up, and propped it against his leg then reached for the front door.

Whap! The door was whipped out of his hand and came to an abrupt stop at the end of two stout chains, one at the top and one at the bottom. Two heavy-duty springs were also attached to the door, and as soon as the gust had passed, the door slammed closed in front of him hard enough to amputate.

Warily, Ansdorfer tried again, this time leaning against the door to hold it and kicking the suitcases through the opening one at a time. Dust and small shards of sand came in with the cold air and ruffled around the small lobby.

The door slammed behind him. The linoleum room was about the size of a bathroom, neat but shopworn. A small space heater glowed next to a Formica counter with a girl slouched behind it. There was a sign with removable plastic letters encased in glass that said, "Welcom to Dansing"

Ansdorfer looked at the clerk. "Hello."

The clerk, probably a high school kid, had been chewing her gum, watching the whole door performance with mild interest and no apparent concern for Ansdorfer's struggle or for hotel hospitality. Now that the show was over, she returned her attention to what looked like a textbook and some homework.

"I have a reservation?" He said it like a question. *Maybe that's not how they say it around here.*

"Yep." The girl slapped a key on the desk. "Two ten, around back, top of the stairs."

"Andrew Ansdorfer?" Again, he said it like a question. *Shouldn't they ask for my name?*

"I figured."

He raised his eyebrows, and she sighed, flipping her textbook facedown. "You're wearing a collar. You must be the new priest. They said your name was Ansdorfer. And"—she pointed to a wall of keys—"there is only one room rented tonight. Who else could you be?"

He smiled. "I can see you're a bright girl."

She looked at him blandly.

He took the keys and nodded slightly, almost bowing. "Thank you."

"Yeah, sure."

He tried again. *Maybe she's one of my flock.* "Is it always windy like this?"

She gave him a pitying look. "You're not from around here, are you?"

He sighed and turned to his luggage, which was coated with a fine layer of dust, and thought about what he was up against and how hard it might be. On the long bus ride, he had been wondering just how much of a finder's fee he should allow himself. *It should be more than a token, considering my effort. Fair is fair.* He felt for the piece of gold, warm with promise.

He turned back to the girl. "Do you have a safe?"

Chapter 14 - Rick

It had not been easy following Fortune, but Rick was feeling pretty good about it. A lot of things had gone his way, and so far, he had been able to improvise pretty well.

First, there was the bus ride. That was an amazing break. After Rick had figured out where the priest was going, he had a nervous time of it. He called a travel agent, pretending he had a family emergency. The lady was very kind and gave him a number of flight options, none of which was quick or cheap.

"South Dakota, huh? That's a toughie." He could hear the clattering of keys on a keyboard. "Well, there are no direct flights, of course, and there's some pretty long layovers. Let's see… I could get you into Omaha or Denver with one connection, or Sioux Falls or Rapid City with three connections… but then you'd have to rent a car or something to get to… what was the name of the town?"

He told her again.

"Dansing. It's not showing up on any of my maps. Well, anyway, you know how to get there once you're on the ground, right?"

"How soon could I get there?"

"Hmmm. The flights leave Philadelphia all the time. The trouble is the connectors. The earliest one that gets into the state would be two a.m. Thursday into Sioux Falls."

More than twenty-four hours.

"How much?"

She told him, and he whistled. "Yikes."

"Well, you could try the old-fashioned way."

"What's that?"

"There's a pretty big bus terminal in Philly. I'm sure there's a bus going there eventually."

It was while he was at the bus terminal that he saw the black hat and coat of the priest, and he knew he was in luck. Rick watched him look at the bus schedule and figured out what route he was on. Then he waited a few minutes, bought the same ticket on the same bus, and sat down on a bench to improvise.

He pulled a ball cap and a hooded sweatshirt out of his duffle bag. Then he bought a cheap pair of sunglasses, a ballpoint pen, and a large cup of coffee, which he drank promptly.

When it came time to board, Rick was at the front of the line, cap low, glasses on, muscling his way to the far back. There was a marine who was not happy being pushed aside and said as much. Rick ignored him, sat down next to the window, and looked outside.

"Hey, buddy, what's your beef?"

Rick let his hands show, the knuckles all doodled with crosses and skulls across the back from the ballpoint pen. It didn't seem to impress the marine, who sat next to him, good and tight, preparing to give some lessons in intimidation.

Rick sighed on the inside, figuring that violence might be a possibility, and let loose the urge that had been building ever since he drank the coffee. Slowly, a dark stain showed at his crotch, spreading out and over his pants, the smell and sight getting the attention of the marine.

"What the hell…?"

Rick grabbed at the wet spot on his pants, getting his hands good and wet, then he reached over and stammered, "S-Sorry, man…"

The marine leaned away, repulsed, and with a snort of disgust, he moved to another seat. Mission accomplished. There Rick sat, chafing in his urine, alone and ignored for well over thirty hours until the bus dropped Ansdorfer in Dansing. Rick watched carefully where he was going.

One mile out of town, Rick put up a rant and ran to the front of the bus, demanding to be let out. The marine was long gone—he'd gotten out in Chicago—but the odor from the back was quickly communicated to the rest of the passengers. The bus driver was happy to let the deranged loony out on a mostly abandoned stretch of road in the middle of nowhere, giving Rick a look that said, Good riddance.

Once free, Rick walked back to Dansing, his pants dry but the odor still strong. He found a bathroom at a gas station, where he locked the door, stripped off his clothes and, using the sink, paper towels, and soap, bathed himself as best he could and cleaned the ink off his hands.

Then he pulled on a pair of black pants and a white western shirt with a collar and added a pair of black suspenders. He was invisible again. Back in the colony, he'd known how seldom townspeople even looked at him, his uniform clothing a sign that said, religious cult.

Now he shambled out of the bathroom, a bland Hutterite wandering through a dusty prairie town— nothing new about that.

Chapter 15 - Stacey

Sleep was one of the few things that Stacey could count on, and even that was turning on him. A man of habit and discipline, Stacey ran his day like a clock: up at five thirty with no alarm, then doing the stretching and exercises that his guardian Otto had taught him all those years ago when he traveled with the carnies.

"Yor body and yor mind and yor soul, iss all vun," Otto had said in that thick accent over and over to him when he was an angry boy. "By vorking your body, you are shpeaking mit your heart vat you kann not say out loud."

The movements were mysterious and strange at first, yet Stacy would stretch and pull and lift and brace himself through the exercises each morning with Otto and soon, body glistening in sweat, find his mind and soul strangely relieved.

That was not so much the case these days. Normally, the exercises would be followed by a few minutes of scripture, then two eggs on toast and a cup of coffee would set him up for the day, but his sleep had been troubled and the dreams disturbing. Vangie was in them. She would be sitting at the kitchen table, as she'd always been when she was alive, only this time there were bags packed by the door, and she was dressed in her traveling clothes.

"Time to go, Stace…"

In those dreams, Stacey would not be an adult but a boy about the same age he was when his mother left him.

"But why?" He was always crying in his dreams, heartbroken.

And each time, Vangie would look at him, eyes serene and untroubled by his tears. "Because it is."

The dreams varied a little bit. Sometimes her father, Virg, was at the table too, drinking coffee and saying nothing. Sometimes it was Otto, eating in his fastidious way, the utensils small in his enormous hands. He too would say nothing. But in all the dreams, Vangie would say it was time to go, never explaining no matter how much he cried or pleaded.

And then he would wake up, troubled and groggy, wondering what the dreams meant.

Maybe it's about the election.

Stacey was outside in his uniform, walking to work, eye on the sky and the weather. He sniffed the air. *Winter's on the way.* The two-block walk to work got him to his office by seven thirty. There, he opened the venetian blinds and looked out the window at the flag then wrote a note about the weather conditions— surprisingly varied over the years—in a journal he kept

on his desk, along with a short list of things he was
working on.

He paused then wrote carefully, "Election
Tomorrow," and thought again. Not much else. All other
things he would normally do were based on him
continuing in his elected position, and there were no
crimes or reports to work on. Just another quiet day. He
looked out the window and sighed, wondering if it was
inappropriate to start packing his stuff right then. No,
better not. *Not yet.*

The phone rang, making him jump a little. It was
Alice Ronseth, who owned the Edge O' Town Motel.
"Hey, Sheriff? Can you come over as soon as you can? I
got a situation here."

Stacey nodded. "Someone causing you trouble?"

"Well, kinda. You better come. I think that new
priest stole something, and I need your help to get it
back."

"Like, what did he steal?"

Her voice was defensive. "It's the point of it, really."

"I understand."

"And stealing's stealing."

Waltraub sighed. "What is missing, Alice?"

A pause. Then, still defensive, she said, "A shower
curtain."

Chapter 16 - Rick

When Rick saw only one light on in the second floor of the motel, he felt a surge of relief. *Fortune, baby, Fortune*. He gathered his thoughts for a bit, rehearsing his plan and trying to think of any obstacles. After a moment he shrugged. *Let's do it*.

He knocked on the door. Rap rap rap—just the right amount of urgency.

Ansdorfer opened the door, and Rick pushed him back through, closing the door behind him.

Back, back, Ansdorfer went, his face working through surprise then recognition until Rick shoved him down and into a beat-up armchair by the window.

"It's you." Ansdorfer clearly didn't remember where he knew Rick from.

Rick decided to help. "From the nursing home."

"Yes!" Now Ansdorfer was just getting around to indignation. "You have no right being…"

Rick took the wind out of his sails. "How about the

rights of the Jewish people and all the things that were stolen from them by your friends the Nazis?" He spat the words out.

Ansdorfer blanched. "What do you mean?"
"Don't bluff me! I've been tracking this Schmidt guy on behalf of the Israeli government for five years. We found him. We know about the gold. And now you suddenly light out of the nursing home like your hair is on fire. Do you know there is no statute of limitations for abetting a war crime?"

The priest's face crumpled into tears, and Rick felt relieved. *He bought it.*

"I-I was only going to find it and give it t-to the Church—"

"The hell you were! The Church office in Philadelphia has no record of why you took this position, and there was no communication with you or from you indicating your real reason for coming here."

"But I-I wasn't sure it was real. I-I thought it was a rumor..."

"You can save your story for the Justice Department. I will be filing my report in the morning."

"Report?" Ansdorfer looked horrified.

Rick sighed and looked out the window for a brief moment, as if thinking, then sighed again. "Look, why don't you tell me everything you know."

Ansdorfer told him—enough that Rick knew it would be harder than he thought. The gold was hidden somewhere in the Corpus Christi Church. No, Ansdorfer did not know where, and yes, he had proof—a small piece of gold that Schmidt had had when he died.

"Where is this gold?"

Something in the way Rick asked the question must have made Ansdorfer suspicious. His eyes narrowed. "It's hidden."

Shit. Rick tried to recover. "Good. We'll get it later." Ansdorfer looked off to his left, and Rick followed his glance. *Under the bed.*

"So tell me, who else have you met with to find this gold?"

"No one! I just got here and checked in."

The desk clerk. Rick pursed his lips. *Didn't think of that.* He looked at the priest carefully, deciding on risks, weighing the reward. He shrugged and stretched a bit as though relaxing after a long chase. He stepped to the window and glanced outside while he fished what he needed out of his pocket.

Ansdorfer was still looking away, shoulders slumped.

Quickly, Rick looped the piece of clothesline over Ansdorfer's neck and pulled up and hard. Each end of the line was tied around a short piece of dowel, making the grip easier. Then it became harder. Rick had never killed anyone before, and it was tougher than it looked. The priest was flopping around, flailing his arms. A lucky shot from the back of his hand caught Rick in the nose and made it water. Fingernails dug into the backs of his hands, deep and hard, scraping bloody grooves into the flesh. *Man, this guy is strong!* With a heaving lunge, Rick raised his arms, twisting around. With his back to his victim and his hands crossed over his chest, Rick bent over, lifting the struggling man up onto his back and off the ground.

Two minutes, maybe longer, the body finally stopped moving.

Muscles trembling, Rick sank to the floor with the corpse next to him, exhausted. The body jerked one last time, and with a farting noise, the bowels released. *Shit!*

Quickly, on his feet again, Rick looked in dismay at the pool of urine spreading out from the body. He could only imagine what else was being purged. *What a mess.* And then there was the even more difficult problem of schlepping this stiff out the door and down the stairs without being seen or causing an even bigger mess.

First the stiff, then the desk clerk.

He went into the bathroom and was washing the blood off the back of his hands when he saw the shower curtain.

Chapter 17 - Katie

Katie Ronseth was Alice Ronseth's granddaughter, probably her favorite. Not that favoritism got her very much except working all the odd hours at the Edge O' Town. If there was as shortage, the phone would ring at home, and sure enough, it was not a cute boy like Derek Hofer—or any boy—but instead it was Grandma Al with a request for help.

"Can you send Katie over right away to turn over rooms?" or "Can you get Katie over here to work the desk tonight?" The demand was phrased as a request, but it never really was. Katie was okay with it mostly.

This was her senior year, and Katie knew deep in her heart that she would not come back to Dansing after her freshman year of college. She loved her grandma and her parents, and her little brother for the most part, and she was wise enough to know that she might even miss them when she was gone.

The tornado that came through town in August had helped her realize that. It took out their garage and scared the heck out of all of them. She realized that night in a very real way that the people and things that she had taken for granted all her life could be snatched away in a single second. So the older and wiser Katie was a little kinder and more patient, even when weird things happened at the front desk.

Such as the Hutterite with the chore gloves. Guy came in after dark, walking right in the glass front door, and scared the heck out of her. He was a big, potato-faced man, wearing suspenders, as they all did, and the black shoes, but this guy had on brand-new yellow chore gloves. *Weird.*

"Hey. You da girl been workin' the desk?"

She eyed him suspiciously. "Yeah."

"Well, der's sometin' wrong out back of your place."

Katie rolled her eyes. *Great.* "Like what?"

The guy just shrugged as though helpless to explain any further.

Typical. *What a moron.*

But since the tornado, she was trying to be more patient. With a heavy sigh, she put her homework aside—American lit books were good, but the lectures were boring—hopped off the stool, and walked around the counter. The guy hardly moved, and Katie had to practically squeeze around him. *Probably a perv.*

He seemed a little jumpy too, which made Katie a little jumpy. When the horn sounded in the front lot, they both jumped a little. *Something wrong with this guy.*

It was her dad in the pickup. "Hey, Katie! Get a move on!"

Normally, such brusque treatment annoyed her, but not this time. Scooping her homework off the counter, she headed out the door and away from the weirdo with the chore gloves.

Her dad didn't seem that impressed either. "Hey." He said it in the general direction of the Hutterite. Then he said to Katie, "Mom's got all the packing done. I'm to pick you up, bring you home, and then we'll head out."

Then he said to the man in the gloves—louder this time, since some of these guys were a little slow—"We got to leave now. Heading to look at colleges with Katie. USD, SDSU—she's up for a scholarship." It was none of the stranger's business, but a proud dad didn't mind sharing that information.

The Hutterite seemed interested. "USD, huh? That's a hike... taking the weekend?"

Then her dad opened up with the whole list. "Nope. Going to Creighton, St. Mary's, then down to USD, up to Brookings, and back through Mitchell and Dakota Wesleyan. Should take about a week." All were good schools, and all had some scholarship offers, but he had bragged about it enough that unless he felt some interest, he kept it to the bigger schools.

By that time, her dad was out of the pickup and helping Katie lock the doors of the motel. Locking a door right in front of someone might seem rude, but her father was a big man with large, rough hands that could practically reach around Katie's waist, and his general presence made people more obedient.

It sure worked on the Hutterite. Not so weird or jumpy anymore, he said it was probably nothing out back, just something he thought they should know about.

Katie's dad paused, then shrugged. "If it's bad enough, you can tell the sheriff. His office is down the way. Sheriff Waltraub is his name."

The Hutterite nodded vaguely. "Well, have a gud trip, then."

Her dad looked at her when she got in the pickup. "He try anything?"

She shrugged, "Nah. Just some weirdo. Harmless."

Chapter 18 - Geist

The list of places, accounts, addresses, descriptions, and passwords had all been memorized. The small green ledger book that contained all the lists had been destroyed, along with the Nazi accountant who'd had it. They were both burned completely and the ashes and bits of bone dispersed along a deserted beach.

Geist was working his way methodically through the list, gathering the riches in order of safety and return on investment. Not as easy as it sounded—it was a puzzle with many variables that made deciding how to order the list intriguing.

The first question was what. "What" might be a priceless work of art, but there were too few collectors to make it safe enough to work with. Yes, Geist knew some names, but those he'd learned while in the Mossad, which meant they would know the names too. Far too risky to stick his head in that noose.

Jewels were an excellent idea, but he would need to do some research before he walked into a bank loaded with security cameras. No, what he was looking for was something easy to find, with little or no security, hiding in plain sight. It needed to be valuable but easily disguised and sold. Silver and gold would be the best.

And of course the country was important too. Some of the security and paranoia surrounding Europe would make transport difficult. The same was true of the Middle East and the communist bloc. No, the best places would be in North America—Canada, Mexico, and the United States, where he would find vast expanses of roads, miles and miles of open borders, and lax security.

He checked a map, where small dot sat in the middle of the vast continent. Centers of security and law enforcement, such as the FBI and CIA, would be thousands of comfortable miles away. He smiled at the thought.

This can go at the top of the list.

Chapter 19 - Stacey

Alice Ronseth was waiting for Stacey, standing in the glass-walled office of her hotel, looking out at him with her hands on her hips as he got out of the cruiser. She was not known to be a patient person.

"Took you long enough." Not a very polite person either.

"Sorry, Alice." Stacey thought about being rude right back, since he was soon to be out of a job, but old habits died hard. He took off his hat and set it on the counter. "How can I help you?"

"Let's go to the crime scene." Alice liked her TV cop shows.

Stacey looked at her. "You mean where the shower curtain was stolen?"

Alice glanced suspiciously back at him to see if he was being sarcastic. He hid it well.

"Let's go."

The crime scene was behind the motel, up on the second floor. Alice led the way up the expanded steel steps at the back of the structure and then on to the weathered-wood landing that stretched along the front of the second-floor rooms. The whole area was exposed to the weather, with steel chairs next to each door along with coffee cans half-filled with sand, in case a lodger wanted to enjoy the fresh air or a smoke. Most of the time, it was too cold, hot, windy, or buggy to enjoy either, so the cans remained empty of butts, and the chairs had a habit of getting blown into a clump at the end of the landing.

Alice kicked one of the chairs aside and pointed to the door with a flourish. The handle had a yellow towel tied around it. "The only yellow thing I got."

Stacey went along with it. He shook a clean handkerchief out of his pocket and opened the door. "Looks okay to me."

Alice ignored him. "The problem is not here—it's in the bathroom." Leading the way across the room, she went into the small bathroom. The linoleum-and-Formica room was dated but clean. The tub stood by itself, a bar along its length, empty.

"Aha." Stacey tried to look impressed.

"Listen, laugh if you want, but I just put new curtains in all the rooms last week. It wouldn't have bothered me if he stole an old one, but brand new? Plus—he's a priest! He's supposed to know better."

"How do you know it was a priest?"

"Cause he booked it that way a week ago, and he signed his name that way last night."

"Maybe someone else took the wrong room."

"He was the only one who checked in."

"Who was at the front desk? You?"

Alice looked defensive. "My granddaughter Kate. She's gone with her folks to look at colleges, so I can't reach her. But she's sharp, that one. If there was anyone else checked in, she would have left a note."

Stacey knew the granddaughter and agreed with the assessment. He guessed again. "Maybe someone broke in with an old key."

"Had the locks changed two months ago, using the insurance money from the tornado."

"Could be a door didn't get closed, and someone walked in."

"Could be you're afraid of getting my shower curtain back."

Stacey looked at her wryly. "It seems a little heavy-handed to bring the full extent of the law into play against a shower curtain. Have you talked to him?"

"That's your job."

Stacey sighed. "All right, I'll go over and see him."

"When?" When Alice Ronseth wanted justice, she wanted it right now.

He raised his hands in defeat. "I'll drive over now."

At first, that seemed to please her, but then her face clouded in thought. "Wait. What happens after tomorrow? I mean, will Darren White follow up?" The whole town was taking the election of Darren as a forgone fact. Sheesh. Thanks, lady.

"Well, assuming Daren wins the election for Dansing County sheriff..." Stacey hoped his sarcasm would make her feel a little guilty for asking.

She didn't take the bait. He sighed and continued. "He will not take office until the second Tuesday in November. That should still give me a good week to mop up this crime spree."

"Good." Only then did Alice smile. "Oh, and fair's fair." Alice paused and reached into her pocket. "This was in the safe with his name on it. He must have forgot it. Once I get my shower curtain, he might as well have it back. I put it in this evidence bag."

The evidence bag dangling from her hand looked more like a Ziploc, but Stacy imagined it would work as well. He stepped closer to look at the... keychain?

No. He hefted it a little. *Looks like a piece of gold.*

*****

The election process in the United States followed a general format but also allowed for a lot of latitude, especially at the local level.

In most areas of the country, county elections took place in the fall, with the actual change in office or law happening the first of the year. Though this was the general rule, individual counties had changed over time, depending on what issues and circumstances arose.

In Dansing County, the issue that arose in the election of 1902 was bad luck. Orval Sagdalen, a rancher from Line, and Orval Doyle, a Dansing shop owner and Civil War veteran, both were running for a vacant seat on the County Commission. Since water rights were a major issue, the election was hotly contested, and the two emerged at the head of a heated race with a high voter turnout.

When the votes were counted, it was a tie, both candidates getting two hundred four votes. Rather than go through the expense of another election, it was decided to pick the winner by luck of the draw.

A crowd gathered at the largest Dansing saloon, where Sagdalen drew a three of hearts and Doyle an eight of clubs. Angry at losing, an allegedly drunk Sagdalen threw a punch at Doyle, breaking his jaw. Doyle demanded an arrest be made, but Herbert Ham, the sheriff at the time, was married to Sagdalen's sister. He had also been defeated for reelection and refused to arrest Sagdalen.

After assuming office, Doyle, a sore winner, used his influence to push for a fast turnover following the election of Dansing County officials. Each incumbent would have only seven days to vacate the office.

Attempts had been made, over the years, to revisit the law and get it changed to something that allowed more time for transition, but there had been no pressing need. That need came later, after the blizzard and what were called the priest murders. But as the old German ranchers said at the café, "Too soon old, too late smart."

Chapter 20 - Herman Deuxcamps

Herman Deuxcamps maintained his sanity through a series of little rituals sprinkled throughout each day. Shortly before seven thirty in the morning, his coffee pot was empty and rinsed out, and he was walking down the tree line of the cemetery, lighting his second cigarette of the day.

He stopped, looked around to make sure no one saw him, and proceeded to take a leak on the stone marked "A. Jackson." Of course, it was not Andrew Jackson, but pissing on it made Deuxcamps feel a little better on behalf of natives everywhere. Sometimes he would piss on a Custer, sometimes a Lincoln—though not often, since Lincoln was a baby who'd died in 1963— sometimes a White or English. The markers would change, but the motives stayed the same: vengeance.

Not that he was in favor of hooking up with AIM or anything. Deuxcamps was deeply conflicted when it came to race. He liked and admired a few white people yet hated all white people. A few white men—his drill sergeant, his Marine buddies, for example—he'd gotten shot at and drunk with, and they gave him the pride and discipline he'd lacked as a youth. But the white man had also systematically destroyed his culture and his people and was the reason they were broken down in the first place.

Herman also loved and respected a few Native friends and relatives and was deeply disgusted with his tribe. His grandmother had taught him some of the old ways, and old Joe DuPree had told his stories of a time when the Lakota were a fierce and feared warrior nation. Those few examples were littered among families where abuse, alcohol, drugs, crime, and corruption were so commonplace that Herman had moved off the rez many years earlier for his sanity. It was much easier to defend his people when he didn't have to witness their activities.

Father Patrick—he was another good one. Herman crossed himself and sent a prayer up to the Great Spirit for the man who had been his white employer for more than thirty years. A long time ago, when he was out of the Marines, he had gotten drunk and punched a redneck because he wanted to. Father Patrick had bailed him out.

Old Virg Sanders, the sheriff at the time, asked why the priest was interested in paying the fine, and Father Patrick said right away, "Because he works for the parish."

The sheriff looked at Herman. "Do you?"

And Herman said, "Yep."

So that was what Herman did. He was young and angry yet also curious and good with his hands, Father

Patrick taught him how to do a lot of things and other ways to behave. Not that much older than Herman, Father Patrick was like a big brother. Over the decades, he'd listened to Herman rage, mentored him in things from prayer to plumbing, defended him passionately when he thought Herman was getting a bad deal, and ultimately became his friend.

But death was part of life, and even though he was sad, Herman carried on without the priest. He even handled the working part of the burial—he marked the grave site, dug the grave, set up the vault and lowering device for the graveside ceremony, and directed the procession to the graveside, where the visiting bishop said the last rites. When they were all gone, Herman lowered the casket into the vault, set the vault lid, and lowered the whole unit into the ground, the heavy lowering device whirring and clacking away. Then he hauled the dirt over with the wagon and tractor, filled and packed it all back in, and seeded it with grass seed.

The cemetery had been deserted by the time the service was finished, so Herman had chanted a holy verse in Lakota for good measure.

The priest was buried between the cemetery workshop and A. Jackson, so Herman added yet another little ritual to his day. Squatting next to the still-bare earth, Herman took a drag on the cigarette and had a little conversation.

"Hey, Father. How ya doin'?" Herman looked up and around. "Still good yet—sun shining, gonna be nice, maybe even hot today, but you can see where it's about to change, huh?" Another drag. "Trainin' that Robert guy in, that guy with the purple mark on his face—the one that showed up after the tornado? Seems like he likes leaning on a shovel more than using it. Not sure I trust him, but then again, he is white."

Herman smiled and sat on an upright marker next door. "You'll be getting your marker in before snow flies. That's kinda pushing it, but Monsignor Morton promised it, so I guess it will happen. Concrete pad is ready anyway." He took a final puff.

"So what's with the new priest, anyway? Talk about strange. He's, like, wandering around in a fog, like he's never been in a church before, asking me all kinds of strange questions, where everything is stored. He's strange all right."

Herman stood up and stretched a bit. His right hip was a bit gimpy. *It's hell getting old.*

"Anyway, I just don't think he'll last long."

Chapter 21 - Stacey

The Corpus Christi Catholic Church was the most impressive building in Dansing County. Built by German Catholics in the early 1900s, it was a marvel of sweat and workmanship. The stone material was easy to find. The entire state of South Dakota consisted of a thin layer of soil on top of a thousand feet of rock. In the case of Corpus Christi, the rock was purple quartzite, massive blocks of it levered into place with ropes and horses, course upon course stretching one hundred ten feet high—almost as high as the elevators by the railroad tracks. Next to it was a matching stone rectory, massive and gloomy, with ten rooms and only one priest to rattle around inside.

Stacey stepped onto the heavy stone porch and into the deep shadows and knocked at the white screen door. The weather was pretty warm for that time of year—the heavy oak door was open, and Stacey could see faintly through the screen into the dim interior.

Not a Catholic, Stacey had never been inside. He liked historic things and would've enjoyed a tour, but considering the reason for his visit, he kept a respectful distance, and his eyes stayed mostly straight ahead.

He heard someone step down the hallway, and then a figure approached through the gloom.

Strange. That was the first thought Stacey had. The priest was a wide-faced, bland sort and stocky, with a strange, tentative expression as if he didn't know where he was or what he was about.

"Y-Yes?"

Stacey consulted his notepad to make sure of the name.

"Father Ansdorfer?"

"Yes?" The eyes shifted to Stacey's badge and gun and then to his boots, making only fleeting contact with Stacey's eyes. He stood about a foot from the closed screen door and made no move to open it. His hands remained at his sides and were wrapped in what looked like gauze.

"You okay?" Stacey motioned to the hands.

The eyes flitted up then down. The hands touched each other. "It's a rash. I have ointment on them."

Stacey nodded, feeling awkward, looking for a way to lead into the topic. "So, ah, you stayed last night at the Edge O' Town?"

The priest's eyes went up and down. "Yes."

"Okay. Well, ah, there's no easy way to say this, but I've had a complaint…"

The eyes flashed up, not tentative this time but almost desperate. "Complaint?"

Taken aback, Stacey looked at him. "The owner is missing a shower curtain."

The eyes flitted again, and this time, a bit of his tongue came out and touched his lip. Definitely strange.

"Oh, I see." He paused again and then said in a rush, "I was worried about this rash being contagious, so I took the curtain."

Stacey was embarrassed. He did not want to know about some sort of weird body rash on a strange priest. "Okay. Well, ah, that's okay. Um, but you did take it, so…"

Quickly, the priest said, "Yes, and I'm terribly sorry. I will replace it as soon as I can." He had a slight German accent, which was understandable. The rumor mill said he was from Pennsylvania.

Stacey was wondering how to end the conversation when he remembered the other item. "Oh, and did you leave this in the safe at the front desk?" He held up the piece of gold in its plastic bag.

The response was immediate and alarming. "Yes!" The priest jolted to the screen door, fumbling for the latch. Taken aback, Stacey took a step back literally and figuratively. *Very strange.*

As the door started to open, Stacey made a spot decision. He put the gold back in his pocket and used his other hand to push the door closed again.

"Say, uh, tell you what—why don't I keep this for safekeeping." He smiled and shrugged an apology. "I mean, until Alice Ronseth gets her shower curtain back."

He sized up the priest and added, "A day won't matter, will it?"

Chapter 22 - Ippy

It had taken some wrangling to get the sheriff—the one she still thought of as the real one—to come in for an interview. He'd rejected all of her suggestions for times and places without much explanation.

No wonder everyone thinks he'll lose. The guy never says anything.

Finally, she got him to commit to a meeting at the studio at eight in the evening. That was past her working time, but at least the studio would be empty. That leering pig, Larry Karl, would be gone, and she could focus on her job.

Ippy looked up at the clock in the lobby of the radio station, which read 7:46.

She sat in a dusty orange upholstered chair across from a dusty green upholstered couch. The lobby was set up to look like a living room from a past decade. The lamp looked like an old-fashioned salon hair dryer. She clicked it on and soon was reading a carefully handwritten instruction manual left by Stan Martin, the guy who used to have her job. It was a simple three-ring binder with "K-D-A-N News Department" written on the spine.

Strange. Everyone seemed to have a Stan Martin story. She shrugged. Small town. *What can you expect?* A guy got involved with a couple of murders, and one of the people killed was a millionaire—people were gonna talk.

In the back lounge area where the jocks hung out, there was a bad photo of one of the victims, a dreamy-eyed kid with a mop of hair. The photo—grainy and off center—was in a black frame and hung over a dent in the paneling. Ippy felt sad whenever she saw it. *Poor kid.*

She shook her head and returned to the manual. This Stan Martin guy was at least meticulous. The tabbed pages contained contacts, addresses, a future file of expected events along with contacts, and an evergreen file of seasonal stories that could be worked year after year. There was also a back section with instructions on how to use the equipment along with idiosyncrasies about every electronic device in the building: "Deck #2—slow capstan, RtoR—brake grabs on rewind."

There was even a very short bio about every public official. Curious, she looked up Waltraub.

"Waltraub, Stacey, Sheriff. Unopposed last two elections. Widowed. Father-in-law was sheriff prior. Private. Seldom comments. Thorough. Will confirm off-record details only. Does not speculate. Poor sound bite."

Hmm. Sounds about right.

Despite the hour, the street in front of the station was bumper to bumper with school kids all driving the same loop, staving off boredom, chores, and homework.

She heard a honk outside and a faint catcall, then, "So long, Sheriff!" followed by a knock on the glass door. There he stood, hat in hand, waiting by the door then pushing the buzzer and peering inside.

Ippy felt a faint rush as she opened the door—nerves probably. She was still learning the art of interviewing someone.

"Hello, Sheriff Waltraub?"

There was another honk, and a kid's voice behind them said, "Sheriff White, baby!"

Waltraub's mustache twisted wryly. "I guess for a while."

"Damned kids."

"Yeah. It's something you gotta get used to. There's always a smartass."

He was bigger than she remembered, not taller but thick and deep. Standing next to him, she could smell a hint of leaf tobacco, hand soap, machine oil, and the outdoor air that still clung to him. She wanted to breathe in more but didn't want to get caught.

When she stepped closer, she could see that he had a weather-beaten look and a drooping gray mustache that made him seem older than he probably was.

She spoke before she thought. "You should shave that mustache."

He looked down at her and raised an eyebrow. "I'll take it under advisement." Then he tilted his head. "Is that why I'm here—for campaign advice?"

"Sorry, none of my business. I sometimes stick my foot in my mouth."

He nodded once, and then the silence grew. Ippy became flustered. "So even though we've met, I might as well make it official. I'm Ippy Johnson, KDAN news director, and I'm collecting interviews from all the candidates for county office. We'll broadcast them in the next week as people make their final decisions about who to vote for."

More silence.

"Is that okay?"

He nodded. "Yep."

This guy's quite a talker.

She led him into the conference room, where the recording equipment was set up. She pulled the curtain closed across the window.

He looked at her.

"Privacy. I don't want any kids on the street rubbernecking as they pass."

He nodded and then sat stiffly down, hands on his knees.

"Relax. This isn't an electric chair. I'm just gonna ask some softball type of questions, basic stuff, like I ask everybody."

He nodded warily, sitting even more erect.

Jeez.

Ippy tried not to roll her eyes. She hit the play and record buttons on the big reel-to-reel deck and tapped each mic to make sure they were hot.

She pointed to the one in front of Waltraub. "Can you give me a level check?"

He looked at it suspiciously and leaned carefully

forward. "Hello?"

Now she did roll her eyes. Exasperated, she reached over and stopped the machine.

"What the hell are you doing? I've been in town for exactly one week and can already see you're twice the guy that slick kid with the teeth is. Is anybody helping you with this election?"

Waltraub shrugged, slightly defiant. "Maybe I don't want the job."

"Well, good for you, because everybody I meet, you included, thinks you won't have it by next Tuesday."

The big man sighed, long and slow. Then he glanced at her with those sad eyes, shrugged, and spilled it. "I got the job only as an accident. Then kept it only to stay close to Vangie. She was the one I later married. Anyway, her dad, Virg Sanders, was the sheriff. Arrested me for vagrancy and fraud when we was passing through town. Vangie sized me up—she had a gift that way—said I would be worth hiring, so he let me out of jail, dropped the charges, and I started working for him."

Ippy cursed herself for stopping the recording machine. Maybe after talking him through, she could record it again.

"How'd you get arrested in the first place?"
"I was a carny, traveling through, like I said. The boss pulled a fast one, skipped town with the money, and because I was part of the act, I couldn't get away and was arrested."

"What was the act?"
"I said I could out-pull a mule."

Ippy waited for an explanation and didn't get one. She prompted him. "You said you could out-pull a mule."

"Yep."

She raised her eyebrows and thought about her Volkswagen. "So that's why you can lift a car. You're a circus strong man?"

He looked a little sheepish. "You'd have found out anyway. People talk about it."

"Can you rip a phone book in half?"

"You mean this?" He reached and lifted up a copy of the Dansing phone book and Yellow Pages. The entire thing was maybe forty pages of cheap, unfinished paper.

She laughed at his expression. "No, I mean, can you still do some of that stuff?"

He studied her for a moment before saying, "Yeah."

She whistled. "Does it help?"

He shrugged. "Sometimes. Like the bar the other day, when I broke that pool cue, that probably saved the crowd getting out of hand."

She remembered and gave a slight shudder. *You ain't kidding, cowboy.* "So where you from, then?"

It was hard to imagine a face getting sadder, but it did. "Ohio somewhere."

She changed the subject. "Are you any good at this job?"

He looked at her, and she rephrased. "I mean, it seems like you'd be good at this job. A lot of it anyway."

He nodded. "Yeah, most of it. I can tell when someone's lying usually or got something to hide. Most of the stuff I do around here is just keeping an eye on the small stuff, encouraging good people to stay good."

"And you don't like…?"

"The paperwork. The laws that sometimes get in the way of what is right and wrong. Virg taught me that. He said 'Do the right thing, and let God decide if it's against the law.'"

"Like breaking that man's hand at the bar."

"Yeah. Seemed a little cleaner way to teach a lesson, rather than involving courts and judges and lawyers. Gotta say"—he glanced at her—"it felt better too."

Thinking about it, she nodded. Yes, it did.

"I can see how that's old-fashioned, maybe even dangerous now. But it's how Virg taught me, and it's the only way I know how."

"Was Virg the one who taught you how to read people?"

"Nope. That is one hundred percent carny. You go from town to town, stranger to stranger, you better learn to read people quick." He paused, more animated than she had seen him. Then he shrugged his shoulders a bit, as though he had made a decision, and held out his hand. "Here, let me show you." He motioned. "Give me your hand."

Hesitant, she offered her right hand.

"Okay, one of the things we did was palm reading. There are a few tricks, but most of it is reading people's faces or how they move or react to what we say."

His hand was huge, almost like a leather mitt. It was calloused, dry, and surprisingly warm. Her hand was tiny in comparison and curled slightly, palm up.

"Okay, here are the lines we read." A large

forefinger traced her palm, making her tingle. *Oh Lord.*

"This one. It goes across the top of your hand. It's called the heart line. It measures your heart, physically." He held it gently. "And emotionally." She felt her face flush. "If you've ever had your heart broken, you can see it…"

He paused, leaned back, sighed, and pulled his hands back away from her. "I'm sorry."

Her heart was beating faster—she could feel it. *He knows.* She had never thought that heartache could be so easily seen but could see now how the right person would be able to read it.

His eyes were sad again. "I'm sorry, miss. I have been using a cheap parlor trick at your loss and expense."

Her mouth was dry. The memory of her past betrayal and the proximity of this man put a lump in her throat that made it hard to speak.

He was on his feet and at the door before she could find her voice. "But what about our interview?"

"Not necessary."

"But what if you lose? What will happen then?"

He looked at her with those sad eyes, his hand on the doorknob. There was a brochure on her desk, a trifold full-color campaign piece featuring a grinning Darren White. He looked at it and shrugged one shoulder. "He'll be fine."

Chapter 23- Geist

The first person on Geist's list lived in a small resort town in about the middle of Minnesota. He had chosen it for efficiency—it was only a day and a half's drive from there to the next name on the list.

Geist drove around town for a bit to get a sense of things. Nothing unusual really. There was a rich part of town by a lake, a poor part of town by some railroad tracks, a pretty good-sized shopping area—they must have drawn shoppers from a fair distance—a movie theater, a couple of museums, a small hospital, an industrial park that catered to agribusiness concerns, and the office of Dr. Lewis H. Brewer, DDS.

He was not surprised, and that was a good thing. *Routine*. The house would not be the best place—too big a chance of security cameras and the like. Work was better, but still, for what he was planning, he needed to be certain that he would have a few hours alone.

It helped that Brewer was a dentist. It also helped that many years had passed, and any worries the dentist might have had about being discovered would have died down. Geist picked a spot near the parking lot of Brewer's office, close enough that he would be driving slowly but far enough away from any cameras.

He found a pay phone and called first, describing his pain, asking for help. The dentist did not ask how he'd gotten his number. When he asked to see him in the morning, Geist gave a terrible moan. Brewer was kind. He agreed to open his office and help him right away.

One block from the office, Geist stepped in front of Brewer's car, a handkerchief with blood on it partially covering his face. Concerned, Brewer stepped out of his car to help. Still moaning in pain, Geist twisted his body and brought his other hand up and around to the base of the man's bare neck. He pulled the trigger, and jolts of electricity shocked the man into rigor.

Smoothly, Geist shoved Brewer back into his own car and pushed him over to the passenger seat. He tossed in a small black attaché case and slid in behind the wheel of the still-idling car.

Within twenty minutes, Brewer was trussed to a chair in a warehouse that stored seed corn. The building had poor security. Geist, with a Richard Nixon mask pulled over his face—he enjoyed a little humor now and then—stated the facts.

Fact one: the very nice Dr. Brewer was the nephew of a very bad man who'd once served in the Gestapo. This very bad man had fled Germany with eighteen bars of stolen Nazi gold, and it had recently been discovered.

Fact two: the security that protected the gold had one weak link, and that was Dr. Brewer himself. This nice, soft man knew code words and tricks to get to the stolen gold.

Fact three: Dr. Brewer was about to find out that Geist was not nice or soft at all and would use pain to extract the information.

Brewer was adamant. He knew nothing about the first two facts. He was a hardworking, loyal citizen of the United States of America, and if Geist dared to try anything…

Geist sighed and interrupted Brewer with a hard backswing with a large crescent wrench he had found in the warehouse shop. His aim was perfect, shattering several of the nice dentist's teeth, and a shower of blood, bone, and teeth arced across the room. No doubt, the nice dentist knew full well how much his mouth was damaged.

Brewer fainted. Geist woke him up with a bucket of cold water. This time, Brewer admitted through broken teeth that his uncle was a Nazi but said that there was no stolen gold. Geist studied the sobbing man with blood and drool spilling down his front. It would do no good to hit him again in the same spot—he might break his jaw, making the dentist harder to understand.

He opened up his attaché case and studied the tools in it, looking for the most persuasive one for the situation, and decided to improvise. Geist took a compressed-air hose, attached to a compressor—the warehouse shop was well equipped—and blasted cold air into Brewer's mouth.

The dentist screamed.

"The exposed nerves must be very sensitive," Geist

said in a concerned tone.

He did it again. The pain must have been intense. Brewer immediately fainted again. Geist threw on more cold water.

Then the helpful Dr. Brewer remembered everything. Gently, Geist cradled the nice dentist's face in his hands and explained a few more facts.

Fact four: the Nazi gold was stolen, and it did not belong to Brewer. Furthermore, the kindly dentist had to realize what a mistake it would be to call the police. That would cause the dentist just as much trouble as if he had stolen it himself.

Fact five: Geist had no interest in harming the dentist any further. In fact, he needed Brewer to live and help cover up the crime. If Brewer was killed, it would cause an investigation that might cause more problems for Geist.

Reassured by the argument, the nice man obediently led Geist to his house. He dismantled the alarm systems, opened the floor safe, and even carried the gold, one bar at a time, to Brewer's pickup, which was brand-new with all the nice features, very comfortable.

Keys in hand, Geist sat in the nice man's truck, almost completely satisfied that the dentist would tell no one.

Almost.

Sighing again, Geist rolled down the window of the truck and reached into the attaché case. He shot Brewer twice in the chest and once in the head.

Finally satisfied, Geist nodded. Now, on to South Dakota.

Chapter 24- Robert

Robert had little memory of the events leading up to the tornado and none of the actual event itself. His first memory was waking up at night in a pasture, cold and naked, without a stitch of clothing on. He had a terrible throbbing where his right ring finger used to be. Blood was caked around the base of the finger and still oozed black in the moonlight. Thirsty and feverish, he'd hobbled barefoot until he found a road.

Three days later, he was released from the hospital with still no real memory of what had happened. A priest had given him clothes and offered him a place to stay and a job. Grateful for that and still shaky about past events, Robert had taken the offer and slowly gained back his memories.

The more he remembered, the less he talked about. The gang he'd ridden with and the life he'd lived didn't seem like the kind of stuff a priest would approve of. Plus, he needed time to think about his life, heal from the nightmare of that horrible day in August, and decide just what his next move should be.

But he was growing bored. His finger had healed over, his strength was back, and he was doing grunt work for a suspicious Indian.

It's time to do something. He woke up in the middle of the night thinking that, not really sure what that meant. He would prowl around the room or maybe take a walk outside, rubbing the stub where the finger used to be, trying to remember more details, trying to recall exactly who he was. The name had come back soon enough, and the things he'd done with the brothers, and even details about his childhood. But what he couldn't quite grasp was the essence of who he was, the man behind the details and facts. It was hard to put into words, but it was like he was blurry, with no real identity of who he was or what his purpose was, and that blurriness bothered him as much as the missing finger, maybe more. So until he figured that part out, he kept getting up at seven, making up his cot in the basement of the rectory, eating his meals with the other cemetery workers, and working a full day under the suspicious eye of that Indian. He kept his eyes open.

One of the things he kept watching was the strange behavior of the new priest. His actions seemed stranger and stranger. Like the night he'd arrived. It was getting close to dark when Robert, as he called himself these days, saw the priest shuffling up the street, carrying his suitcase with the sort of run-walk of a person who is out of shape and in a hurry.

Robert was raking leaves underneath the cottonwood behind the rectory, just about done for the day, when he spotted him. Curious, Robert stopped and watched him as he trotted right past the front door and headed to the shed where the cemetery truck was parked. After peering in the window, the priest set down his suitcase and tried the door. It was unlocked, of course, and so was the pickup, an ancient but well-maintained flatbed with the keys in the ignition.

The garage door was lifted open and the priest was halfway in the cab by the time Robert walked over.

"You the new priest, Father?"

The guy about jumped out of his skin, wheeling around with a trapped look on his wide, sweaty face. "Yes!"

Jeez. Robert raised his hands defensively. "Sorry, just thought I'd introduce myself—I'm Robert. Father Patrick hired me to work here at the cemetery."

The priest nodded, not looking at him. "Yes, I see. I'm sorry, my son, but I need to go get my other bags."

"I can go get them for you."

"No." The priest shook his head.

Robert stood and waited for more explanation. There was none. The new priest fired up the pickup and backed out of the garage. Robert had to step out of the way.

Weird. Robert watched him drive out, tires spinning on the gravel driveway overgrown with weeds. He shrugged. The Indian was still inside, waiting for a phone call to go pick up the new priest. Shaking his head, Robert started walking to the rectory back door to tell him the news.

The Indian—Robert didn't like him much, so he refused to use his name—asked more questions. Why had he run there on foot, way across town, instead of calling? Why was he carrying one suitcase and leaving the others?

Robert shrugged and lifted his hands. "How should I know?"

He'd left the Indian standing on the back stoop, glaring after him with his hands on his hips like it was his fault the new priest was a nutjob.

Robert put the rake in the shed. It was past sunset, and he was done for the day. He had no interest in hanging around to see when the weird priest would come back.

Weird is right.

He shook his head at the image of a priest jogging down the street with a suitcase. And why was he wearing chore gloves?

Week Two

Chapter 25 - Stacey

Dansing County's lone sheriff's vehicle was the ponderous old Power Wagon. It rumbled heavily, the only traffic at eight in the morning on Main Street in Dansing.

Rush hour, which lasted about four minutes and offered no congestion whatsoever, was done by a quarter to eight. Stacey rubbed his eyes and stifled a yawn. KDAN was on in the truck radio. Larry Karl was ending the morning news, explaining that yesterday's newly elected sheriff Darren White was going to stop by and talk football. Irritated, Stacey reached over and shut it off.

He sighed and wondered if maybe he should grab a pack of cigarettes. That irritated him more. *Damn things never let you go.*

His mind wandered back to the night at the radio station and talking to the girl. Ippy. She was not a girl

anymore, for sure, but at the dimly lit station, he could
see both the fine lines around her eyes and mouth that
said woman and the humorous tilt to her lips and sea-
blue eyes that said girl.

He shouldn't have held her hand. That stuff about
reading people he could have mentioned without holding
it, but in truth, he wanted to. The hands were what he
thought they would be— soft and strong and matter-of-
fact and capable.

He started whistling absentmindedly then stopped,
embarrassed, when he recognized the tune. "The Girl
From Ipanema."

Dammit.

And that was the real reason he was out of sorts. He
hadn't slept well the past few nights. Sleep usually was
not a problem for Stacey, but there he was at three in the
morning, staring at the ceiling, thinking of that stupid
song and feeling guilty.

It was Vangie who made him feel that way. That was
her favorite song, and having this beautiful woman with
the same name made the song about her and not Vangie.
As wrong as that was, he still found himself thinking
about her and that night, remembering the feel of her
hand in his, watching the pulse beat at the base of her
wrist while he traced his finger gently across her palm...

Dammit!

He made a left off of Main Street into the Edge O'
Town Motel parking lot, where he could see Alice
Ronseth waiting. Stacey pulled in and put the truck in
park. The door opened with a squeak. Stacey had been
planning on getting a can of WD-40, but since the

election, he thought the hell with it.

"Thanks for waiting, Alice."

"You gonna sell that to the new sheriff?"

"Nope."

She nodded as she turned and started walking around to the back of the motel. "Yeah, I didn't think so. He probably doesn't want it anyway." Her keys jangled as she pulled them out of her pocket. Not a sentimental person, Alice did not seem in the least disturbed by the change in office and offered no condolences on his loss.

Even though he'd be out of a job in exactly one week, Stacey couldn't quite say he was sorry about it either. Oh well. Down to business. "When's the last time you switched out your locks?"

"Like I said, after the tornado. Rolled it into the insurance claim. Got a list of all the people who rented that room since, if you want it." She looked hopeful.

Stacey started to say something about it just being a shower curtain, but he had a niggling feeling about the way the priest had acted that made him keep his mouth shut. "Sure, I'll get it later."

She nodded again as she took the yellow plastic bag off the door handle. With an elaborate move, she took a large white handkerchief out of her pocket and opened the door. She seemed to be enjoying it.

"Have you heard from your granddaughter yet?

"Nope, and they didn't leave much of an itinerary, either. I made some calls to the colleges I know they were looking at, but nobody is answering the phone or seems real interested in helping me."

Stacey nodded. His experience with getting help

from colleges had amounted to the same—not a lot of pressing desire to help a long-distance caller.

The door open, Alice used the same handkerchief to turn on the light. The room had the stale look and odor of all motel rooms. Stacy stood in the doorway and looked for… what?

It looked like about a million other motel rooms. This one was down at the bottom as far as amenities were concerned, but it was neat, and they were in Dansing after all. A guy could go broke running a fancy hotel. Few people could afford that, and not that many needed even a cheap place to stay.

"Whatcha lookin for?" Alice was at his elbow.

"I'll let you know when I find it." Feeling slightly foolish, Waltraub pulled a pair of latex gloves out of his pocket, put them on, and did a close examination, starting on the floor and working his way up. It didn't take long. The room consisted of one bed, a phone on a side table, a coin-operated TV on a bracket on the far wall, and two Norman Rockwell prints in cheap frames screwed into the wall. Next to the TV was a closet with a broken clasp. In it were a vacuum cleaner and some cleaning supplies.

There was not much more in the bathroom, just a small sink, a tub with a missing shower curtain, and a toilet.

"Whaddya think?"

Stacey motioned to the closet. "That clasp on the closet always been broken?"

Alice nodded. "Yep. I was thinking of adding that in with the shower curtain, but I didn't."

Stacey didn't say anything, mainly because there was nothing to talk about. Nothing was out of place, nothing looked strange or abnormal. Stacey went through the motions, walking around the room, peering closely into nooks and crannies for… what's this?

Relieved that he'd found something, Stacey knelt down by the side of the bed and peered down by the wall. There was what looked like a piece of paper stuck behind the molding near where the phone was.

His fingers were far too large and blunt to grasp the paper, so he took out his clasp knife and used the blade to worry the piece of paper out from behind the molding. It was the size of a business card—it looked like an appointment card you might get from a dentist or maybe a claim ticket from a repair shop.

"What is it?" Alice was at his elbow again like an ill-mannered dog, her nose about six inches from the piece of paper.

"Well, Alice, I don't know yet." He couldn't hide the tinge of exasperation from his voice. He stood up and looked at the card, front and back. "It's in German, whatever it is."

Alice was obviously having a high old time. "German! What's it say?"

"Don't know."

"Oh." She didn't move, eyes focused on the card like a bird dog.

"Tell you what, Alice. Why don't you lock this place back up again, and I'll go see if I can find some answers about this card."

Alice looked hopeful. "You know someone who can

read German?"

Stacey put the card in his shirt pocket, took off his gloves, and nodded.

"Yep."

Chapter 26 - Greta

It was pushing three o'clock, and Greta was sitting in her usual spot on her tulip-backed spring-steel motel chair, absorbing what sun she could before winter set in for good. Normally, she would sit and talk to Jimmy and watch the shadows move around the yard with the sun, but that day, she had vengeance on her mind.

Greta lived outside of Dansing by the radio tower, on about three acres of land. The amount of land was not really important since it was directly adjacent to a vast stretch of prairie that reached out beyond vision. Her place consisted of a house made out of sod and mud, called a soddy by the older folks. It had a new tin roof, replaced after the tornado, and the same old junk strewed across the backyard, only more battered and tossed around than before the cyclone.

Greta had not been home when the tornado hit, which was lucky. She'd been in town, helping get rid of a body. That was unlucky, but with age, she had gotten more philosophical.

Except when it came to her chickens. She used to have six, and now she was down to three. The first was gone during the night, probably taken by a weasel, but what could you do except maybe sleep in the coop with them? But the last two had been killed in the light of day, an affront to her pride, so there she waited with the Mauser sniper rifle Jimmy had brought back from the war. She was wrapped in a blanket for when the sun started to go down, since her old bones were not as good at keeping the cold out as they used to be.

Darlin'?

"What?"

Sheriff is comin'.

"Dammit!"

Jimmy had a habit of showing up whenever he felt like it, and it didn't do any good to yell at him or pout. He just kept on being Jimmy—tall and lean and forever young, all sun and blue sky, not a bit of guile or meanness in him.

She, on the other hand, had withered over time and gotten tough like a piece of dried leather.

"What's he want?"

Jimmy didn't say anything, which again was typical. He made her so mad at times she couldn't see straight. Then he'd disappear for a while, so she'd get lonely. When she just about couldn't stand it, he'd show up at night, his warmth and presence as real and comforting as it had been when he was alive. He'd whisper sweet things and promise her that soon, soon they would be together again.

Inside her house and above the stove on a cluttered

shelf was a small wooden cigar box. She had taken the cigars out after Jimmy died, replaced the contents, and written, "Home" on the outside. Many evenings, she would sit by the stove and hold the box in her lap with tears running down her face and a yearning in her heart. Home was Jimmy, and with him gone, the winters were especially lonely. She thought about the box and wondered if she might use it soon.

Her expression softened, then she sighed. Jimmy. Greta tilted the Mauser down and took the cartridges out. The varmint would have to wait for vengeance. If Jimmy said the sheriff was coming, it had to be important.

Chapter 27 - Stacey

Stacey had had many dealings with Greta over the years, and his opinion was a mixture of admiration and uneasiness. Admiration because she was salty and tough and about the size of a small boy, with white hair cut short and faded blue eyes. And uneasiness because she had a way of looking at him through those eyes and smiling a secret smile as if she knew him better than he knew himself.

"Not sleepin' well, huh, Sheriff?" She was sitting in the passenger seat of his truck with a small smirk on her face.

"I sleep fine."

The smile again. "Uh-huh."

It gave him the creepy-crawlies. When he pulled up to her house and was about to get out of the truck and walk to her door, the passenger door opened, and she hopped right in, saying, "It's time to go. Let's get this over."

"Go where? Get what over?"

She rolled her eyes with disgust. "You men." She leveled her eyes. "You been stuck for a long time. It's time you got unstuck." Before he could ask what she was talking about, she motioned with her hand. "Jimmy said you needed some help, so let's get goin'."

Jimmy was her dead husband. He'd died a long time ago, but she talked about him all the time. People in town thought she was crazy, and maybe she was, but crazy or not, she often seemed to know things that were good to know. That was another reason he drove out to see her.

"I just need you to read something. It's in German."

She pondered that with lips pursed then shook her head. "Nope. It's more than that. Let's go."

She gestured impatiently again, flipping her hands forward with a shooing motion. "C'mon."

Stacey put the truck in gear and set his jaw. "You know, I'm done bein' sheriff next Tuesday. Who you gonna push around then?"

She smiled sweetly. "It looks like Darren White."

He shook his head. "And good luck to him." To say it out loud gave him a sense of relief. *Maybe it's just as well*. He fished out the card. "Here. Can you read this?"

She took the card from his hand and studied it back and front. "Yep."

"Well?"

"I'll tell you more when I see where you got it from."

He said no more and avoided eye contact as much as possible. Nevertheless, on the drive to the motel with her in the passenger seat, he felt as if she were reading his soul like the morning newspaper.

Fortunately, Alice Ronseth was out on an errand, and the teenager at the front desk, another grandchild, passed over the key with a bored look and zero interest. Alone, Stacey unlocked the motel room again and motioned Greta inside.

She walked in and sniffed. "Bleach."

Stacey sniffed. "I don't smell anything."

Greta rolled her eyes. "No surprise there." Quick, like a curious little boy, she darted around the room, lifting up the bedspread and getting down on her hands and knees. She finally sat on the toilet, looking up and around with a satisfied air. "Yep."

Stacey was standing next to her in the bathroom, "Yep, what?"

She nodded. "Something strange all right. It's everywhere, especially here."

Stacey looked around. "I don't see anything."

"I know!" Greta had a triumphant look. "That's what I mean."

Stacey looked at her, waiting her out.

Greta gave in. "Okay, I'll show you." She walked into the bedroom. "See how clean it is? There's no dust, there's no smudges—even the floor's been vacuumed. See how the carpet strands are stood up? Who vacuums a rug before they leave a motel room?"

She got down on her hands and knees and set her eyes down low. "See? Lookit in the corner under the desk. No dust on the carpet." She slapped down with her hand, whap, whap, to prove the point. "You might go two, three months before you'd see a person vacuum under a desk nobody uses, but there's no dust. And here." She lifted the chair and pointed underneath. "No gum, no smudges."

She sniffed the underside of the chair. "Smells like bleach. You never use that on wood chairs. Too hard on the finish. And lemme check..." She walked over to the closet with the broken clasp and opened it. "See? No bleach in here. No motel in their right mind would stock bleach in a closet. Too easy to spill and damage the upholstery and carpet."

Then she pushed Stacey to make him sit down on the stool in the bathroom.

"Look around. See any smudges? Feel under the lip of the sink... feel anything sticky, like old toothpaste or mouthwash that collects there? And the floor... looks like someone went after the cracks in the linoleum with a toothbrush."

Stacey scratched his head. "Yeah, I suppose you got a point..."

"Prove it to yourself. Ask for a key to any other room. If they're anywhere near this clean, I'll eat a straw hat."

"What about the card?"

She laughed. "It's a catechism card, the kind you give kids to help them learn verses, only it's in German. It looks like it's been in someone's wallet for a while. See how grimy it is?"

"What's the verse?"

"Revelation 21:21: 'And the street of the city was pure gold, as it were transparent glass.'"

"Gold, huh?" His hand closed around the piece of

gold in his pocket.

She looked up at him, eyes narrowed. "You gonna tell me what this is really all about?"

It was Stacey's turn to smile sweetly. "Nope."

Chapter 28- Rick

Seven days in, it was not going well. Rick rubbed at the backs of his hands, which were healing from the scratches left by the dead priest. They were itchy but still tender enough that he kept them covered with bandages and some white gloves he'd found in a drawer in the rectory.

Taking a breather from his search, he sat at the table in the kitchen with a pot of coffee and some NoDoz and ran down the list of good and bad things. First, the good things. Nobody had figured it out yet. Sure, they were suspicious about the way he had helped himself to the cemetery flatbed, the gloved hands, and all that. But the dead priest was pretty close to the same size as him, so the clothes fit okay, plus he was a priest now and entitled to a little authority. He was able to declare no services for Saturday and Sunday. A time for prayer and preparation, he'd said. Looks were exchanged, but no one spoke up.

The next good thing: because he was a priest, he had

the rectory to himself. He dismissed the maid and other volunteers, saying he was deep in prayer, so he was able to spend time searching the whole place without causing any raised eyebrows, even rooting around in the basement when the cemetery workers were on the grounds.

The last good thing, and really the best one, was being able to get rid of the priest's body with no problems. No one saw him roll the body down the steps of the motel or steal the bleach out of the gas station restroom. No one seemed to be missing the fifty-five-gallon drum sitting across the alley, and most impressively, no one had noticed him drive back to the cemetery with the flatbed and the drum on the back.

It would have been easiest to leave the drum on the back of the truck, but that Indian and the guy with the blotched face and missing finger were far too nosy, so he was able to rassle the drum into the rectory then down the hall into his bedroom closet. He dumped a bag of kitty litter into the drum and sealed it. The closet was a large one you could walk into, with a window for light. He'd opened the window an inch or two to keep the temperature down.

Rick had sore muscles and scratches but no real emotions tied to the murder. "Murder." He whispered the word out loud, checking to see if there would be a twinge of guilt.

Nope. He shrugged. He thought he might be more emotional about it, but it was surprisingly easy. Another thing to add to the good list—you never knew when you might need the skill again.

Now it was time to run through the bad things, and
first on the list was that he could not find the gold. Yet.
He had been through the whole rectory, from the
basement and cellar to the attic, knocking on walls and
floors, moving rugs, checking in the back of closets for
hidden panels. All he found that was useful was a packet
of white gloves in the dining room and a little bottle of
NoDoz in the kitchen. He did find a dusty bottle of
booze in the cellar, but it was empty.

Second on the list was that he was definitely running
out of time. The weather was still pretty nice for
November but cool enough that the body in the drum
was not too smelly yet, and there was plenty of incense
to mask things until… Saturday.

Saturday he would be expected to hold his Mass.
There was no way he could get out of it, and he was sure
that more than the usual number would be there out of
curiosity. Plus, there was no doubt that the sheriff would
be poking around. Rick could tell that the way he'd
reacted to the piece of gold had made the sheriff
suspicious.

I should have pretended I never saw it. Oh well.

Saturday. He had three days to find it. He paused at
the temptation to wait longer but shook his head. *Too
risky*.

He had to take the search over to the church building
itself. No doubt, people would notice and ask questions,
but it couldn't be helped. His hands shook a bit as he
poured himself some coffee and tossed in a few NoDoz,
making himself jittery with adrenaline and caffeine.

No rest for the wicked.

Chapter 29 - Janet Hofer

Janet Hofer was the seventh of nine Kleinsasser girls. Four of the sisters had married Hofers, and between the two clans, they populated about half of Dansing County and about two-thirds of the Corpus Christi congregation. Janet was the coordinator for the Daughters of the Nile. She was also on the funeral-service committee for handling funeral lunches and the kitchen committee for all other meals served out of the basement of the church and was general master sergeant for all things involving the parish.

Janet and her far meeker husband, Ray, had nine children of their own and plans for at least one nun and one priest out of the brood. But as devout as she was, Janet was fast developing the opinion that the new priest, Father Andrew, was a weirdo.

First, there was daily confession. True, Janet was a once-a-weeker, but it stood to reason that she should come and confess something to the new priest, so there she was on a Monday, eight in the morning, and the church door was locked.

Undeterred, she went knocking on the rectory door and found that locked too. It took a good ten minutes of hefty pounding for the door to be opened and a bland-faced man with bleary eyes to appear, staring out through the screen of the storm door. He was looking at her shoes. His eyes only flitted up for a moment while he spoke, and then they looked down again.

"What?"

Big, loud, and brash, Janet was seldom without an opinion or a word, but she was so taken aback that her mouth fell open and nothing came out.

Still looking at her shoes, he started closing the door and had gotten it most of the way shut when she blurted, "Wait!"

He stopped closing the door but did not open it back up either. He stared down through a six-inch gap.

"I'm here for confession." She pointed over to the locked church.

His eyes went up, then down again. "I've been praying for all of you and have been seeking guidance."

Click. The door closed in her face.

Two days later, she was more prepared. CCD classes were every Wednesday, so she brought her key and let herself in through the church basement. CCD was not her deal—Helen Schaumeit handled that—but he didn't need to know that, the weirdo. Praying was one thing, but if he thought he was going to blow off teaching the next generation of believers...

She stomped up the steps from the basement, gearing up for the confrontation.

Nothing. The office was empty. The sanctuary was empty. The side storage room where Father Peter used to hide was deserted too.

Weirdo. She sat down with a huff on a front pew. The statue of Mary stared down at her. She looked sympathetic.

While Janet was commiserating with the sainted mother, she heard a faint sound, or maybe felt it more than heard it. She stood and tried to locate it, moving forward, up the three steps that led to the altar, and then off to the left side. The noise was coming from the closet that held all of the banners and altar cloths. She opened it and stepped in. As far as closets went, it was a pretty big one. It even had a small stained glass window that gave some light into its cluttered interior. There was the new priest, standing on a chair and knocking on the paneling, facing away from her.

"What are you looking for?"

He jumped and almost fell off the chair. Catching himself, he wheeled around with a mixed expression of guilt and fury.

The look lasted for only a split second but was long enough to cause her to involuntarily step back.

He composed himself. If he recognized her from the other day, he didn't mention it. He cleared his throat. "I am looking for old records."

She raised an eyebrow and pointed to some leather-bound ledgers next to his feet. "You mean these?"

He paused. "Yes. And some others as well."

Man, this guy was weird. "What for?"

He said nothing but got down off the chair. He was

medium height, kind of stocky, with a plain potato face. He didn't look dangerous, but something about him made Janet feel uncomfortable.

"Excuse me. Who are you?"

"Janet Hofer."

"Well, Mrs. Hofer. I can see that this is bothering you. I will take these documents and continue my search later."

"What would you want with old cemetery records?"

He paused. "Part of my charge is to know the history of this church, not just the living but the dead."

"Well, that ain't all of them. These books are only for the ones buried since"—she looked at the spine of one of the older ledgers—"1945."

He stopped and looked at her then up and to the left as if thinking. Then all of a sudden, his eyes got bright, and his smile grew wide. "Mrs. Hofer. I do not have my glasses with me. Perhaps you could help with some of the fine print."

She shrugged and opened one of the ledgers.

"Well. Like you can see, these are all written by hand. And because you never know who will die and when they will die, the ledger has twenty-six, like, chapters, one for each letter of the alphabet. So you pick a letter, like, say... B."

She flipped the pages over the thumb-marked B. "See, there were about a page and a half of Bs. They go from Axel Brandt—my husband's second cousin's husband, buried in section H, row two, plot three, buried on April fourth, 1945—all the way down to the Baker baby. She didn't have a name, just the Baker baby. Poor soul, died November third, 1977."

She pointed to a newer version of the same type of ledger. "After that we got a different ledger book. It's about half-full. So you find who you're looking for either by knowing the year and last name of the person who died or by knowing where they're buried and finding their tombstone."

She turned and lifted a hinged piece of Masonite out from next to a file cabinet. She unfolded it like a Monopoly board and pointed to a series of small rectangles with faded names written in most of them. "This is the map of the cemetery. Herman Deuxcamps is the one who keeps the records."

"So you could come back and find a... loved one very quickly, even after many years." The priest seemed excited about the thought.

She gave him a secret glance. *Weirdo*.

Chapter 30 - Rick

Rick was back at the rectory with the leather-bound ledger open on the kitchen table, the enormity of the task dawning on him. He had paged through the book and located each date between 1944 and 1945. There were nine names.

Nine. The problems were obvious. It would take a good half day apiece to dig down to each grave enough to see if it was a body or gold. That meant four and a half days, and he did not have that much time. If he knew how to run the cemetery backhoe, he could easily do it in a day and a half, but he didn't. And even if he could, there was no way he could do it without rousing suspicion. He was getting too much notice from the Indian, the sheriff, the loud woman, and the guy with the missing finger, not to mention the countless looks and comments from townspeople.

Yes, he had stayed hidden in the rectory and church as much as he could, but people still found a way to get in his path and... look. The attention was obvious. His iron-haired secretary with eyes like flint had even set a note on his office desk with a flourish. "It's the bishop's office."

"I see," he'd said then looked at her until she left, her face set in a scowl.

Now he was back hiding in the rectory, and the note was lying next to the ledger. He did not have to read it to know what it said. "You're running out of time, buddy."

Two days. Maybe two and a half. He could feel Fortune slipping around him, sidling out the door and down the road. *Not so fast, bitch.*

He had no really good options, and he knew that if he were to get any chance in getting the gold, he would have to tell someone else—a huge risk but unavoidable. And that made the choice also unavoidable. He would have to trust the guy with the purple face and the missing finger. What was his name—Robert?

First of all, Robert had spent some time on the inside. There was a way of behaving that the ex-cons had. It was hard to miss. He had no idea what Robert's history was like, but Rick felt he might surely be open to the thought of finding gold. Second, he knew how to run the backhoe on the tractor. Rick had seen him messing with a trench out by the back of the property. Third was that Rick felt pretty confident that he was smarter than Robert. If he handled things right, he might not have to share any of the gold. No need to tell him about all of it—just tell him there was four hundred pounds. That was enough.

He rubbed the backs of his hands absentmindedly. At that moment, the stately grandfather clock in the hallway chimed the quarter hour. *Time to go.*

Nodding with decision, he adjusted his collar and bandages and headed off to find Robert.

Chapter 31 - Herman Deuxcamps

It was eleven at night. Normally, by this time, Herman had finished his work for the day, watched a little TV— very little, since you could only get two channels in Dansing, and both of those were pretty staticky—and went to bed.

He sat out on the small cement pad in back of his kitchen door, in a lawn chair, staring out at the cemetery.

Gold?

Robert had come to him a few hours earlier and said he wanted to talk about the new priest.

"Yeah?"

"I don't think he's a priest." It was then that Robert explained about the meeting with the priest, the possibility of stolen Nazi gold from World War II sitting in some grave in Dansing, South Dakota.

The more surreal the story sounded, the more attractive it became. Robert leaned in, his voice edged with excitement. "I mean, why not? It would sure explain him acting so strange—snooping around like he was looking for something."

Herman's voice was dry. "A lot of things would explain that better than gold from World War Two."

Robert was not deterred. "Listen. All we gotta do is help this guy, keep our eyes open, and see what happens, okay?"

"Why're you tellin' me?"

"You know why. You don't trust me much, and you don't trust him either. If I didn't tell you, you'd figure out something was up and probably tell Sheriff Waltraub."

Herman shrugged. That was true enough. "How much gold does he say there is?"

Robert's eyes were feverish, and his voice dropped to an excited whisper. "Millions. He figures there's a couple hundred pounds."

Two hundred pounds? Figuring that gold was roughly a thousand bucks an ounce… yeah, that was a lot of money.

Herman licked his lips in thought. "Why do you think he's not a priest?"

Robert leaned in a little. "He can't read."

Herman raised his brows, and Robert rushed on. "I used to run with"—he paused—"a rougher crowd. Some of them couldn't read or write. They were real good at covering it, so you couldn't hardly tell, but you get so you can figure it out, and I'm almost certain that new priest can't read. And"—he sat back and raised his chin in defiance—"when's the last time you saw a priest that couldn't read?"

Chapter 32- Stacey

Pheasant season was winding down. The birds were still out there, but the threat of an any-day-now blizzard had cut down the number of out-of-state hunters to a straggling few, mostly northerners who weren't bothered by a little snow. The days were a little schizophrenic— cold in the morning, with frost on the windshield of the truck, and afternoons hot enough to roll down the window and wish for a little AC.

Stacey eased the Dodge down onto the creek bed. Shifting low, he powered his way up the other side, the heavy truck creaking a bit as it climbed its way out and up onto the sparse and weedy plateau littered with tumbleweeds and the cluttered homesite beyond.

In front of a low sod house stood a figure, waving to him with a casual air.

Hyram Fassbender looked just like a prospector was supposed to look, with a gray beard that started up under his eyes and ended around the beltline of a pair of faded Levis. In a nod to the current era, he wore a pair of nylon hiking boots and a ripstop nylon camo jacket and had a forty-foot antenna guyed up over his sod house.

While Stacey parked the truck, the prospector walked over to the milk crate by the front door of the house, a beat-up tin mess kit in his hands. "Hey, Sheriff."

"Hyram."

Hyram lived in and around and near some federal grazing land and was technically a squatter, trespassing on government land. But because the boundary wasn't very clear, and because Hyram was harmless to man and land, Stacey let him be.

"Sorry about the vote."

Stacey shrugged. Hyram had said the same thing a few days earlier when Stacey dropped off the chunk of gold. There was nothing else to add.

Since he had time, Stacey found a rusted milk crate, dusted it off, and sat next to Hyram, propping himself next to the soddy's doorway. He motioned to a stack of wood that stretched along the side of the house and rose to just under the eaves. "Think you got enough?"

Hyram nodded. "Yep, these soddies are pretty well insulated. I figure it at an R value of fifty, plus the K value you get with the mass of the sod walls. Once snow starts to drift in, that all increases." Hyram was a geology professor who'd retired from an Ivy League school while still in his thirties. He spent his summers looking for gemstones and his winters reading crime novels, a contented man.

Stacey eased back against the wall and sighed. This was a peaceful place, and he didn't want to add any turmoil. Finally he spoke. "So I talked a little to Darren White, you know, about this." He motioned around him at what was probably an illegal settlement. "Told him you could be of help. He said he'd keep it in mind." He wasn't optimistic about this.

Hyram sighed. "Yeah, I get it." He paused and gave a wry smile under his beard. "It's been good while it lasted."

Stacey sighed with him. "Yeah, I know what you mean." After Vangie died, Stacey had spent more than a few evenings sitting around Hyram's place. The quiet presence of the prospector had made his grief and loneliness easier to bear.

Hyram broke the silence. "Anyway, I got some data on your sample." He motioned inside. Stacey stepped into the unusual interior——a neat white-walled room that looked like a state-of-the-art laboratory and did not match its rustic exterior. In the corner, a military-style cot, a small kitchen, and a large bookshelf were the only signs of comfort. The rest of the room looked like a research lab. About six years earlier, Hyram had found a meteorite somewhere and sold it for a hefty sum then used the proceeds to pay for all the equipment. Stacey knew enough about prospecting to know that it was a feast-or-famine business and, on average, most prospectors lived just on the edge of poverty. He was glad that Hyram had beaten the odds.

"Here you go." Fassbender handed Stacey his piece of gold back in a clear plastic bag with a twist tie and a neatly lettered card attached to it. "I wrote the percentages down. It's gold all right. And it was definitely refined, because it's not irregular like a nugget out of the ground would be, and when I did the analysis, there were none of the trace elements you would find in a melted-down nugget."

Stacey held the nugget and looked at the card. "Sixty-seven percent gold, thirty-three percent silver." He raised his eyes to the prospector. "Is that normal?"

"I'd say mostly no." Fassbender shrugged and ran his hand through his thinning hair. "I'd have guessed it was chiseled off a larger gold bar. See where the chisel mark is and then where it broke loose? If it was a gold bar, you'd normally think it was part of a gold ingot or bar like the kind you read about at Fort Knox. But if that was the case, it'd be ninety-nine point nine nine percent pure. This is only two-thirds gold."

"You think someone was trying to pull a fast one, maybe water down the product?"

The miner waggled his hand, undecided. "Maybe. Or it was a gold alloy for a specific purpose."

"What kind of purpose uses one-third silver, two-thirds gold?"

Fassbender smiled. "You don't see it much now, but back in the day, it was used a lot." He tapped an incisor. "For teeth."

"Teeth?" Stacey looked surprised. "And this was chiseled off a bigger bar?"

The prospector nodded.

"So, like, this was part of a bigger bar that a dentist might have had?"

Fassbender's smile was wicked. "Or maybe it was melted-down teeth he got after the fact."

Stacey frowned. "That ain't funny, Hyram. You mean like the Nazis?"

Fassbender shrugged. "That'd be a lot of teeth."

Chapter 33 - Geist

The Sioux Falls Regional Airport was a study in lax security. It was fascinating for Geist to compare the difference he had seen in his travels. In parts of Europe and the Middle East, soldiers with machine guns searched bags with guard dogs on alert and security cameras on every post.

Here, half a world away, crime and terrorism seemed a forgotten concept. No one was concerned about him or his shotgun in the camo carrying bag slung over his shoulder. Another hunter dressed in matching camo saw him, recognized the gun, and waved, saying, "I left some for ya."

An airport staff member stood at a booth with tourist information and looked laid back and friendly. No one requested ID or asked why he was there in South Dakota.

The only one who even noticed him was the apologetic counter person at the car rental center, who set down a paperback to help him and asked for his driver's license. "Sorry, they make us check this stuff."

Geist smiled and gently waved the inconvenience away with his hand.

"So, Mr. Porter"—the clerk confirmed the name— "you've got a spanking-new F-150, loaded, and a seven-day, unlimited-mile rental agreement. Just sign here."

Geist signed and pocketed the keys in the quiet, forgettable way that was his trademark.

The clerk had mostly forgotten him already and was reaching for his paperback when he threw off a polite question. "So you going hunting?"

Geist smiled. "Yes, I am."

Chapter 34 - Robert

Robert felt for the pillowcase underneath his cot, trying to decide the risks, weighing the pros and the cons. Had he been presented with the idea of finding stolen gold just a few months earlier, he would have sworn off the whole thing. The frightening night of the tornado had literally scared the hell out of him. Large chunks of his memory were still missing from that night, but enough remained to haunt his nightmares.

But that was then. The memories had started to come back, bit by bit, so that now he could remember the life—the feeling of riding wild and free, the motorcycle hammering a tune up his spine, the horizon calling his name.

He was just a few weeks from heading south anyway. He had a thin roll of bills, some earned, some pilfered, enough to get out and hide from the harsh weather someplace where he could cook in the sun a little while he figured things out.

But with the priest whom he was now certain was a fake, he had a chance to make a play big enough to buy a fleet of bikes and maybe even a whole island down by the keys. He remembered talking to a guy who'd done okay for himself doing some smuggling—drugs, handguns, that kind of stuff—saying the money was easy and the life was carefree. Shit, he wouldn't have to lift a finger. The amount of gold they were talking about could keep him in beer and women until he was ninety, smuggling or not.

It was dark, and Robert was alone. Feeling safe, he pulled out the bundle and unwrapped the gun. He'd bought it off a guy at the bar in town who'd had the look, and sure enough, he'd had what Robert needed.

The shyster seemed to know how much he had, too, taking him for one hundred thirty bucks for a piece-of-shit Saturday night special and a box of bullets. The thing had cheap chrome that had mostly flaked off and a stubby little barrel good for close work only. But that was okay. If he figured it right, the sight of all that gold would be enough of a distraction for two quick shots for disabling and four more carefully aimed shots to make absolutely sure.

Thinking a bit, Robert bundled the gun back inside the pillowcase and put it back under the mattress. He rubbed the nub of his finger at the base of the palm where it had been plucked off in the storm. The scar was still angry and red, and the fingertip that was no longer there still throbbed and itched. Scratching the tips of the other fingers, Robert eventually fell asleep with a small smile on his face.

Chapter 35- Herman Deuxcamps

It was two in the morning, and Herman Deuxcamps couldn't sleep. Sighing, he rolled off his cot, pulled on his boots, and reached for his lighter and his smokes. Leaving the light off, he shrugged on his beat-up leather jacket and walked out the back door onto the little concrete stoop. There he stopped and squinted as he lit up his first cigarette of the day. He breathed in deeply and relaxed. *Damn things.* He thought about quitting many times a day but liked it too much.

Herman pocketed his lighter and went out into the moonlight to piss on A. Jackson and gather his thoughts. The air was pretty calm for South Dakota, with a light breeze and temperatures around the freezing mark. He shivered a little as he watched the stream arc and steam onto the granite marker. Then he took a puff and asked a question of his old friend.

"What do you think they're up to, Father Patrick?"

He pondered each of them—first, the strange new priest, then Robert, the one with the missing finger.

"Yeah, you're right. They're both snakes." But that was not why he hadn't been able to sleep. Distrusting white men was a daily activity and one he did not lose sleep over. He frowned as he wrestled with the real reason.

The gold.

He found himself thinking about it and wondering just how much of it to believe. It did make sense, in a way, but he wasn't sure if it actually made sense that a bunch of Nazis would hide stolen gold in a Catholic cemetery in Dansing or whether he wanted it to make sense.

Two hundred pounds. That was a lot of gold. He found himself trying to guess just how much that might be worth, and no matter how he figured it, it added up to millions. Millions. A guy could do a lot out here with a couple of million dollars in gold. No doubt at all that those two bastards would try and cheat him and that he should keep an eye out, maybe see if he could beat the greedy white man at his own game.

He paused to stub out the cigarette. He had thought he might talk to Father, see what he had to say, but he just couldn't stop thinking about the gold and whether it was real and how he might get to it without getting tricked or killed.

He walked back toward the house, lips moving, thoughts whirring, his conversation with Father Patrick unfinished.

Chapter 36 - Monty Cooper

Monty Cooper was driving aimlessly through the north side of Dansing, late afternoon, not paying attention to anything but the turmoil inside his head. He had just gotten his insurance check from the damage to his funeral home, and although it was nice, it was not nice enough.

Cooper and Son Funeral Home had only two real issues that made it hard doing business. The first was that his bloodsucking father had sold the business to him for way more than it was worth, pulling a snow job on him and the bank, convincing them both that the funeral business in Dansing, South Dakota, was destined to prosper and that Monty was easily capable of making the steep loan payments to the bank. Having accomplished this, the elder Cooper had headed south to Pilot Point with his latest wife and had never been heard from again.

The second real issue was that Monty Cooper was no businessman, and after years of mismanagement, he was looking for a way out, driving his limping hearse through the back parts of town, casting about for ideas that might work.

Arson. Monty tapped the steering wheel of the hearse with one finger nervously while he chewed on a thumbnail, thinking, thinking, thinking of how he could actually do it. The trouble was, he didn't know exactly if he had fire insurance.

He thought he did. It made sense that he would, right? He had even asked his insurance agent for a new printout of his policy, but the damn thing might as well have been written in Chinese for how understandable it was. The next step would be calling his dad or his agent and fishing around the topic, but even Monty could see that would not be a good idea.

Hey, Jimbo! It's Monty Cooper. Say, if my funeral parlor was to suddenly burn down, how much money would I get?

He sighed, staring gloomily out in front of the hearse as it eased by the Catholic church and cemetery. His eye caught some movement off to the side. He looked, looked again, and then slammed on the brakes.

What the hell?

He pulled the hearse to the curb and jumped out, leaving the door open and the engine running. There in the middle of the cemetery were the old tractor and backhoe with Herman Deuxcamps behind the wheel, lifting an ancient concrete vault up and out of the ground. Next to him stood what must have been the new priest, and next to him was the fella that had showed up after the tornado, the one with the missing finger and blotched face, named Richard or Robert or whatever.

Next to him, which had made Monty slam on the brakes in the first place, were five—no, six!—other vaults lying out along the ground.

As he approached, he could see the three of them shooting looks back and forth like third graders caught passing notes in class.

Monty was out of breath and angry. "Herman! What the fu…" He noticed the priest and changed his language. "What the heck is going on here?"

It was cold, and Monty's breath came out in puffs of steam. In his astonishment, he had left his coat in the hearse, and he was starting to feel the wind bite through his suit coat.

Herman's nicotine-stained smile looked forced. "Hey, Monty. Just disinterring some graves by order of the diocese." He shrugged like it was no big deal, just some guys out working in the cemetery.

Monty's mouth was open, and he did not know where to start. "How many?"

"Nine."

"*Nine?*"

The priest and the Richard-Robert guy shrugged along with Henry.

Nine. Yep. Just another day in the cemetery.

"So where is the licensed funeral director to oversee all this?" Hands on hips, Monty watched them look at each other.

Herman started. "Well, this is consecrated ground."

Monty raised his voice, "What the fu… what does that have to do with anything? South Dakota state law says you gotta have a licensed funeral director oversee all disinterments." For a man who moments before had seriously been considering arson, he felt surprisingly indignant about this.

All the sudden, a suspicion formed, and he stopped and pointed at the vaults on the ground. "Are you using the Croftons?"

The three said nothing. Monty hated the Crofton brothers with every nerve in his body. They ran a funeral home in the neighboring county and had the unmitigated gall to assume they had the right to do funerals in his county. The glances between the three made him more certain.

Hands on hips, he asked the question again. "Are you using the fucking Crofton brothers?" Their silence confirmed their guilt. "I can not believe that you are using fucking Eddie and fucking Cal-fucking-Crofton to do nine disinterments in fucking Dansing!"

His pointed finger trembled with rage. "We'll see what the state board of funeral directors says about this!" The three stood and stared at him like cardboard cutouts.

Morons. He wheeled and stalked off, swearing and shouting, until another thought brought him to a halt.

Turning, he pointed to the new priest with one last threat. "And if you think I'm buying a table at the next Knights of Columbus wild-game feed, you can fucking forget it!"

Chapter 37 - Geist

He sat in the local café at the counter on the end, blending in as he always did, an invisible hunter passing through. He had found out what he needed to know and had decided that tonight was the night to act. It shouldn't take too long. He sipped at his coffee and was about ready to slip out the door when he saw the man out of the corner of his eye.

"So where're you from?"

He looked up into the face of a gray-haired man in a cowboy hat leaning against the counter next to him as though they were long-lost buddies.

He stalled. "Excuse me?"

The man smiled wider. "Name's Henry. I ranch west of town." He held out a hand. Dumbstruck, Geist shook it as he stood up from the counter. He had no choice that wouldn't cause more attention. Avoiding eye contact, he decided to play the shy out-of-towner.

"So where ya from?" the nosy cowboy asked again. "You look a lot like Del's nephew, Rolly. Even got a truck like him."

Now three more ranchers were interested, each looking up from the table where the cowboy named Henry had sat.

Geist tried a smile. *Smile and get out.* "Well, I'd know him if I saw him, I guess." He tried to dodge around to the counter.

The one at the table called out in satisfaction, "So you *are* from Sioux Falls."

Geist stuck with the truth. "It's a rental. I'm not from Sioux Falls."

"Of course he's not from Sioux Falls," scoffed Henry. "See, if he was from Sioux Falls, he'd know about the number one on the license." He turned to Geist and said, in a kinder tone, "You see, all plates that begin with number one are from Minnehaha County… Sioux Falls."

By that point, all the ranchers were standing in a half circle, blocking his way to the door. He needed to get out. Now.

Geist repeated, "It's a rental."

"Good," said the third rancher. "I hate those east-river bastards. Runnin' the whole state like it's their personal property."

"But you're from an even bigger city." Henry was nodding as if it all made sense.

Head down, Geist walked toward the till, willing the ranchers to step back.

One of them did. This rancher turned his focus to Henry. "How do you know he's from a city?"

Henry smiled wide. "'Cause lookit! He locked the

door of the truck. You can see it from here. No one does that unless they're from a big city where crooks and drug dealers steal 'em. Plus, his hand was soft when I shook it. He's got a nice rig he rented and some new hunting clothes. He's probably a doctor or lawyer or something, arn'cha? Rolly, he's an architect."

This was bad, bad, bad. Geist's stock in trade was invisibility. For years he had wandered the streets of major cities unnoticed, and now he was noticed. It made him very uncomfortable.

Ignoring the ranchers, he left a bill on the counter and headed out the door.

"Man, you sure look like my nephew. Thought for sure it was him comin' in at first," a rancher called out after him.

He beat a hasty retreat to the truck, unlocked it, and hopped inside.

Shit. He stared ahead, wondering what had just happened. In this, of all places, he felt completely exposed. He took a deep, calming breath, trying to relax.

Rap, rap, rap! There was a pounding on his window. A waitress in white stood shivering in the bitter wind. "Hey, mister! You forgot your change!" She held out the ten-dollar bill he'd left.

"Keep it." He kept the window up, but she must have read his lips.

"But it's ten dollars!" She frowned with concern.

"It's okay." He stepped on the gas and sped away, leaving her behind in the middle of the street.

In his rearview mirror, he could see her still looking concerned, her lips moving, looking for all the world like she was memorizing his license plate. Minutes later, he was back on the road, driving the speed limit, fighting the urge to push the pedal to the floor, heading back to the protection of civilization and faceless crime.

Geist shook his head in awe of his biggest fear, the thing he had just narrowly escaped—recognition.

He pulled over at a rest stop near Rapid City to think about his options.

Chapter 38 - Stacey

Stacey looked up from his cup of coffee and the small stack of handwritten notes and sighed. He was half an hour into two equally draining tasks and was already exhausted.

One was sorting through the file drawer behind his desk. It was a massive steel case about five feet tall, quite probably bulletproof, purchased by Stacey for two dollars at an army surplus auction. The top file drawer had a tarnished brass cardholder in its center that held a yellow index card with the current year printed in Stacey's cramped handwriting. The second through fourth file drawers went back in time year by year to the bottom drawer.

At the end of each year, the contents of each file drawer were moved down the line. The bottom file was then emptied into a banker's box and moved down the hall to the back shelf of the janitor's closet in the jailhouse, leaving Stacy a brand-new drawer to fill in with the year's activity.

Twelve boxes were stacked in that closet, each with a different year, each with his handwriting on the front. Never organized in the conventional sense, Stacey's file system was based on a deep mistrust of anything computer related and a habit of filing everything in chronologic order. Each drawer held twelve accordion files, one for each month of the year. In each accordion file, individual manila folders held issues or crimes or accidents.

As the crime progressed through time, the file would also advance until it was resolved or until it ran out of leads. The file would finally come to rest in the closet, parked permanently in Stacey's personal and professional timeline.

There was no alphabetical order. There was no separation between the personal and the professional— there were just neat files that documented and sorted the life of Stacey Waltraub, sheriff, and Stacey Waltraub, person.

Up until that point, Stacey's year-end organization had merely involved emptying the bottom file into a box and moving it down the hall. But that day, he realized that he would have to explain his system to Darren White, which was depressing because he now saw how amateurish it was, a system that only worked for one person.

When Virg was alive, there was no file or system. The old man simply knew everyone and everything that happened in Dansing County and acted accordingly. After his death, Stacey wrote down some notes on the calendar each day to help him remember things, and those notes had grown to files and file drawers, and those had grown into boxes of files—and the sum total of all that would be laughed at by a man with Darren's training. He could see that now.

But the far more heart-wrenching task was the second: Stacey realized he would need to go through all of the boxes year by year and remove Vangie from them.

It had seemed so natural at first to add her handwritten notes to the files. Many were suggestions of what her father would do in a given situation, where he might have gotten an answer or found a person who could tell him something. Those notes were written in her distinctive bold handwriting, signed with a V, sometimes with a heart after that and other times with a Bible verse.

Vangie's notes had been added to the files, and over time, they'd accumulated and changed from facts and lists to notes of endearment and encouragement, many of them sent along with a homemade lunch, some of them with spots of grease from ham sandwiches or bits of mayonnaise. These he would add, without thinking, to files of vandalism or accidents or missing livestock, all because it had happened on the same day or week.

And now he had to rip his two lives apart, file by file, year by year, until the personal and the professional were separated. He looked at the small stack of notes and felt the urge to pick them up and smell them, to catch the lingering scent of Vangie's perfume that no doubt still clung to them.

Now what do I do?

His thoughts were interrupted by a knock at the door.

Chapter 39 - Monty

Monty was surprised to hear an answer to his knock. Normally, the sheriff was not in his office, and if he was, the door would be open. He had only knocked as a way to let out some steam. He was still hot about the disinterred graves at the church cemetery.

He jumped a little when he heard the sheriff's voice, a muffled bass behind the door. "Yeah?"

He opened it in time to see Waltraub sweep a small stack of papers into the middle drawer of his desk.

"You got a minute, Sheriff?"

Waltraub pulled out a massive red handkerchief and blew his nose. His eyes looked watery.

"You okay?"

"Yeah. Just a cold. Winter's coming. You wanna sit?"

Monty was too amped up to sit, so he told the sheriff about what he'd seen at the cemetery, ending with, "Shit—pardon my French, Sheriff—they can't do that, can they? I mean, unless you know something I don't know. You didn't let those Croftons come into my county"—he paused looking for support—"our county and dig up a bunch of bodies, did you?"

Waltraub rocked back, and the old-fashioned wooden office chair squealed in protest. "Nope." He studied Monty, pale eyes focusing on the problem, making Monty feel a little uncomfortable. "I don't know every law in the state." He motioned to a shelf containing dusty volumes of South Dakota Codified Law. "And these books are about thirty years old. You sure about the digging up of graves?"

"Sure am. They talked about it at the last state funeral director convention in Sioux Falls. They were more talking about Minnesota and Iowa poaching across state lines, but the law is what it is all over the state."

Waltraub nodded. "Well, I'll go check it out tomorrow, Monty. I'll let you know."

Monty felt a bit deflated. "Shouldn't I come along?"

Waltraub was up on his feet and pulling on his leather coat, one made of inside-out sheepskin that made him appear even thicker than he was, like a mournful bear with a mustache. "Nah, that's okay, Monty. I'll head over there first thing tomorrow and let you know."

"Why not today?"

"Been a long day, Monty. I'm tired, and to be truthful, my heart ain't in it. Let me get some sleep, and I'll do it tomorrow first thing."

Monty was about to say something about duty and doing your job when Waltraub paused a bit at the door. "Say, uh, Monty?"

Monty looked at him.

The sheriff shrugged a bit. "Small-town rumors, you understand. Anyway, I was at a state meeting for sheriff departments myself a few months back, kinda like your meeting you're talking about. Anyway, they did a full day training on spotting arson, how to tell how it was done and who the most likely suspect was. Turns out it was almost always someone looking for insurance money."

His eyes were pale and unblinking.

Monty looked back, trying to match his stare. "Huh."

The sheriff nodded. "Just thought you'd find that interesting."

Chapter 40 - Rick

Rick watched the guy stomp back to his hearse and breathed a silent sigh of relief. *That was close.* And that was the problem. Everything was getting close. Decisions had to be made on the fly, and lies had to be thought up on the spur of the moment—stories and alibis that were dangerously thin, but what else could he do?

With each minute that passed, it seemed more likely that Fortune was going to sneak past him and take off with all that gold. But even as time was running out, he felt that he was still in control of things. Just a few more hours—one day, tops—and he would be free and clear and rich. Meanwhile, he needed help from the two cemetery workers, and for that, he needed to keep his cool.

"Who was that?" Rick spoke softly with a minimum of movement in case the guy with the hearse should happen to look back. He was a ways off by then, slamming the door of his hearse and then fishtailing out and down the street. Silly certainly. There was no way the guy could hear, but it sure had been a close call. Rick's hand was in his coat pocket, and he forced his grip on the handgun to relax.

The Indian—Herman? Henry?—answered. "That's Monty Cooper. He owns the funeral parlor in town. Kind of a screw-up."

"Was he right about the state law?"

Herman shrugged. "Probably. If he is, he's the only one who cares about it. Maybe we should move these out of sight before he comes back with reinforcements. Out of sight, out of mind."

Rick nodded. It was hard to file a complaint about what you couldn't see. As far as the holes in the ground were concerned, who cared? It was a cemetery.

"Where?" The worker with the missing finger seemed a little jumpy, a little eager. In the cold air, the blotch on his face looked almost black. Rick thought he was the riskier one of the two.

"Go and open the shop door wide. I'll lift these vaults with the tractor and back 'em in. It'll be tight, but I can stack 'em up inside, then we can see what we got."

The shop was about fifty yards away. The one-fingered worker backed up a few steps then wheeled and ran, zigzagging between the stones, glancing behind himself every few yards like a guy who was expecting to get shot at.

Rick looked over at the Indian and gave a shrug and a smile as if to say, What's his deal?

The Indian smiled back, the cold smile of a poker player. Rick changed his mind. The Indian was definitely the more dangerous.

It took about five minutes per trip. The Indian looped the cable through the notches at the corners of the vaults then hoisted each vault, gently swinging it into the air and, with little jounces, down the slightly uneven ground into the shop. He was concentrating, seemingly unconcerned about either Rick or the one-fingered worker or perhaps confident that they needed him.

Forty-five minutes later, the sky was dark, bits of snow falling sideways in a driving wind. Henry or Herman or whatever his name was hopped off the tractor with the last vault still gently swinging in the darkness of the shop, a single light from the ceiling casting long and dim shadows.

Rick reached into his pocket, not really caring who he hit, just looking for the best shot. He turned and decided on the Indian standing by the door.

Click. The light went out. At the same time, with a loud bang and a flash of light to his right, the muzzle flash of a gun went off. Reacting, Rick wheeled and shot twice where he had seen the muzzle flash. Bang! Again, he heard the same gun but lower, as if it were near the ground. Twice more, Rick shot. Then, slipping to the left, down and away, he crouched low and waited.

It took a while for the ringing in his ears to diminish. There it was—the gasping gurgle of a man shot in the chest. He must have caught the one-fingered man with a lung shot.

So far, so good.

Slipping off his shoes, he eased to the left, away from where he remembered the light being.

Click. The light went on, followed by a shot—

bang!—wide to the left. The Indian son of a bitch then switched off the light but not before Rick could see the vault still swinging gently by its cable. Crouching low, he sidled his way toward the protection of the vault, looking to put it between himself and the shots.

In the pitch-black room, Rick lifted his free hand, groping for the vault somewhere in the darkness, heart hammering away in his chest. It surprised him—it was closer than he thought, catching him in the upper chest near his right shoulder. He reached for it with his free hand, steadying it. Crouching along its length, Rick could feel its rough texture. He smelled the earth as he eased along its side up toward the tractor, ears straining for any possible noise.

He sensed a movement, recoiled, and fired at the same time, instinctively using the protection of the vault as his shield. He did not realize until it was too late that the Indian was already standing by the back of the tractor and the movement he'd seen was around some of its levers.

The ratcheting of gears let loose was almost simultaneous with a horrible shooting pain in the lower thigh of his left leg as the vault fell down, crushing him very briefly into a squat and then horribly twisting him down and into the ground. His left leg was splayed and broken, pinned underneath the vault.

He cried out in surprise and shock. He felt more than heard the crunching. The pain was more of a realization of what must have happened than an actual sensation. A panicky feeling welled up in him along with a cold sense of shock. He tried jerking back and away from the vault, pushing against the rough surface, still not fully aware of his predicament.

Click. The light was on again. He could not see the actual bulb from where he was, nor could he locate the Indian. There was silence while he tried to jerk his leg free. Instant pain clouded his vision and made him gasp.

"Well, well." The voice was behind him. Rick twisted around with his gun and caught a quick glimpse of the Indian's head ducking back behind the vault. "Well, it's just the two of us now. Ol' Robert is bled out, and it looks like you're not too good yourself." The voice was conversational, only about six feet away around the back corner of the vault, completely safe and out of range.

Rick's hand on the gun was greasy with sweat and shaking with pain and adrenaline. He groaned with a mixture of pain, anger, and frustration. "Come help me. Please?"

The laugh was mocking. "Are you kidding? You still got one, maybe two shots. I forget. And who knows? Maybe you got another clip I don't know about. No, I figure I got you pinned now. I'll just wait."

A wave of nausea touched with fear came over Rick. "What about the gold? Doncha want to know where it is?"

More laughter. "I figure it's right here. I got some time to see if it is. If it ain't, I'll just keep my eyes open. Uh-oh. Lookit there. Is that blood on the ground? Sweet Jesus, it is. You musta clipped an artery when the vault pinned ya. You won't last long now."

Rick looked down. Sure enough, he could see a slick

of blood pooling down, spurting with the rhythm of his heartbeat. He could see Fortune turn her back as his vision started to fade. Angry, he shot his gun at the back of the tractor, hoping for a lucky ricochet. One round, bang! Then came the click, click of the firing pin on an empty chamber.

The laughter became derisive.

Cold and shivering, Rick let the gun slip out of his hand. It's not fair.

He thought about Fortune. *Stupid bitch*.

Chapter 41 - Janet Hofer

Janet Hofer was not used to not getting her way. She glowered at Violet Hofer, a Schaumeit married to her husband's brother, Klaus, and a perpetual thorn in her side. Violet was the church secretary, a small, compact woman who over the years had migrated from someone who made passive-aggressive comments to a full-on bitch.

"I said, I. Don't. Know. Where. He. Is." She bit off each word and spat it out, leaning into her desk.

"He's the priest, for God's sake! You're the church secretary. Your job is to know where he is."

"And I said, I don't know where he is, *Janet*." Her mouth soured on her name as though it tasted rotten.

"Well, *Violet*," Janet mimicked, "can you at least tell me when you last saw him? Or would that be too much trouble?"

"What do you need him for?"

None of your damn business. "I found this plat book for the cemetery. He was doing some research on some people buried, but I don't think he saw this." He was a weirdo, all right, but he was the priest. If she acted right in these first days, she could be the power behind the throne, and her first bit of business would be the ouster of one Violet Hofer as church secretary.

"He's not in the office."

"Is he in the church?" There was no answer. "Is he in the cemetery?"

Violet gave a slight turn of the head.

"Is he anywhere in town?"

Violet had moved to the desk and was ignoring her, aggressively shuffling papers into manila folders and manila folders into army-green files.

"What, am I supposed to file a missing person report with the sheriff?"

Violet looked up with sharp glee. "Oh, you'd like to file a report with Darren White, wouldn't you? Why don't you just run over there now and see if he's in, maybe go out for a drink and discuss things."

The shot went home. Janet flushed. Not a fast thinker, she had no good witty comment that would wipe the smirk off Violet's face.

Still flushed, Janet raised her chin. "Maybe I will."

Chapter 42 - Darren White

Darren White pulled into the church cemetery very slowly. He drove a brand-new white pickup with an extended cab and a bed liner, four-wheel drive, custom rims, the works. He traded it in every year without fail, picking up the best and letting his grandpa handle the details with the trade-in and payment.

He was a stickler about his trucks. He hated driving anyplace where dirt or gravel could mar the mirror-bright finish, and the grass and gravel of cemetery roads were suspect. Darren stopped the truck, checked his hair in the mirror, and reached for the bulky plat book Janet Hofer had dropped off earlier.

Janet had been his babysitter back in the day, his first crush. When he was fifteen, they'd had a little summer fling. Back then, she was twenty-five, bored with her husband, Ray, and still had a figure.

Now the figure was gone, but the way she'd looked at him when she handed him the plat book made him think that she was still up for the fling.

He smirked at the mirror. Doubtful.

Fling aside, the plat book was interesting and a way for him to ease his curiosity. There had been comments about the graves dug up in the cemetery, and although he was not yet sheriff and it probably wasn't his jurisdiction anyway, it did make him wonder what that new priest was up to. Now that he was soon-to-be sheriff, it felt good to be able to investigate whatever he wanted to for whatever reason he cared to indulge.

He hefted the book into a gloved hand and stepped out of the heated cab into the late-fall air. *Getting cold.* He zipped up his lined jean jacket, adjusted his cowboy hat just so—a winter-white Stetson with a platted leather band, a congratulations gift from his grandfather—and waited by the truck.

Herman Deuxcamps was just finishing up with some tractor work. He swung down off the tractor and walked over.

"Herman, you look like shit."

"Yeah, long night." His eyes were bloodshot, and he looked exhausted.

Darren waited to see if Herman might add an explanation. He didn't.

"What's going on?" He motioned to the fresh piles of dirt over several graves.

"Not sure. Father Andrew said dig up these certain graves, and then he said put 'em back."

Darren raised an eyebrow, and the Indian shrugged back.

"Where is he now?"

Herman shrugged again. "Don't know that either.

Haven't seen him around. Did you check around town?"

Darren didn't care that much. "What, do I look like the sheriff?"

They shared a laugh.

"Not yet anyway." Herman nodded to the plat book. "Whatcha got?"

"Guess it's an old plat book. Janet Hofer found it in the church—said Father Andrew was looking for old records like this."

Herman frowned a bit. "We got copies of platted ground in the shop. Can I see?"

Darren opened the heavy book up on the hood of his truck. "Looks like a cemetery map."

Herman nodded. "Yeah, we got the same thing in the shop, pretty much. I didn't know there was a copy."

"Well, it's yours now. Can you make sure Father Andrew gets it?"

Herman took the book and gave a lopsided smile. "Sure can."

Chapter 43 - Stacey

That night, Stacey Waltraub had a dream. Exhausted, he
had skipped his careful routine of supper, stretching,
exercise, and a bit of reading, and instead, he'd gone
straight to bed. Kicking off his boots, Stacey dumped his
coat on the floor and fell back onto the pillow. It was as
if all the pain of losing Vangie had doubled back and
combined with him losing his job, and all of it was
pushing down on him with a heavy weight of
helplessness and depression and loss. He closed his eyes
and was asleep.

   In his dream, Vangie sat at the kitchen table. The
window over the sink was open, and a fresh breeze was
billowing out the curtains. She was smiling impishly and
motioning to the chair across from her. There was no
sign of illness. She was fresh and vibrant and full of life
and looked to be the same age as when they'd first met
all those days ago. On top of the fridge was the radio
they'd gotten when they were married. It was playing,
"The Girl from Ipanema," and Vangie was humming

along with the song the way she always did.

"Vangie?" The dream was so real, the colors so vibrant that he could smell the scent of cut grass blowing in from outside. He pressed his palms into the faded red Formica tabletop then looked at his hands and turned them over, studying them. He knew it was a dream but just could not find proof of it.

"Sit down, hon."

He sat at the table and reached for her hands, only then realizing that hers were the hands of youth and his were the hands of middle age.

She gently cupped one of his in hers and held it. "You are a good husband, like I knew you would be."

Her words made him smile. He could feel the weight and sorrow lift from his shoulders. Her eyes were clear, and the small lines around the edges of them creased as she smiled. He found himself laughing, and she joined in.

"Why are you here?" He didn't want to ask—he wanted to just stay in her presence—but he could not help himself.

Her laughter changed to a gentle smile. "'Cause, darlin', it's time to go." She motioned, and there at the edge of a table was a suitcase, the old-fashioned kind with black alligator hide and worn leather straps and buckles.

He wanted to be afraid, to be agitated, but he wasn't. Holding her hand, smelling the lilies of the valley scent she wore, looking at her eyes so bright and serene, everything seemed peaceful.

He took a deep breath and let it out. With that,

tension and worry lifted. He did it again. And again.
With each breath, he felt himself relax more. There,
holding her hand, it felt like… heaven.

"Is this what it's like?"

She didn't answer, just nodded to the suitcase again.
"It's time to go."

Now he felt only curiosity. "Where are you going?"

"Not me." She nodded to the suitcase, and then, with
a smaller nod, she motioned to the radio. "You."

And then he was awake. He still had a smile on his
face and, completely relaxed, he looked around his
room, more rested than he could ever remember being.
Curious, his eyes swept the room, noticing how different
things were without Vangie in them. The room that had
been a sanctuary, the place where Vangie had lived,
seemed dead and empty. He sniffed tentatively. No smell
of perfume or grass, just cleaning supplies and dust. Like
a tomb.

It's time to go.

The dream was fading, but the sentence was still
clear. Still relaxed, Stacey found himself looking at the
things in the room with a sense of detachment he had not
felt before.

Within ten minutes, he had loaded up all twelve of
the bankers' boxes in the back of the Power Wagon and
was heading out to the edge of town where the
abandoned elevators were.

An old dumpster, rusted out and forgotten, sat on
cracked concrete. He looked inside and saw just a couple
of beer cans. Slowly and deliberately, he filled the
dumpster with the boxes and then added some gas from

a small can. He flicked out his Zippo—a gift from his friend and mentor, Otto—lit a piece of partially crumpled paper, and tossed it in.

Woom! Crackling flames lifted up bright and hot, making Stacey step back a few feet. Ten minutes passed. He reached in with a two-by-four and stirred it up, then again, and then again, until nothing but black-and-gray ashes remained. He saw someone who looked like Bob Schaumeit drive by slowly, curious no doubt, but he didn't stop.

Facing the dumpster, Stacey felt his sorrows carried away, bit by bit, as if the ashes held a measurable part of his grief and were taking it from him. He gave a final stir with the two-by-four, to make sure it was all consumed. Then he tossed the board into the dumpster and turned back to the truck with a sense of finality.

It's time to go.

Chapter 44 - Randy Kalani

Looking back on it, Randy Kalani realized the November blizzard might have been more predictable if it weren't for the damn barbwire fence.

Kalani was so sick of answering the question of why he'd moved to Aberdeen, South Dakota, from his native Honolulu that he'd had a T-shirt printed a number of years back with the caption, "Because I Like the Weather."

Even then, it took some explaining. Kalani was a weather nut. Ever since he was a kid, he'd been fascinated with wind and rain and snow and isobars and isotherms. And every day, he grew up watching the same eighty-degree days with sunshine and occasional afternoon showers.

After he got his degree in meteorology, he finally landed his dream job: National Weather Meteorologist in Aberdeen. Day after day, Kalani got to examine and study and wonder at the vastly different kinds of weather that blew by his station.

That day was another extreme example. He was explaining the launch to a high school kid named Brent Johnson, who was looking for some extra credit for his science class. Brent was getting his money's worth from the exuberant Kalani.

Kalani pointed to the small Styrofoam-and-plastic box in his hand. "This is called a radiosonde. It weighs about a pound and has a transmitter in it. When it goes up with the balloon"—Kalani pointed to the deflated beige blob on the floor of the weather station garage—"it sends temperature, pressure, and relative humidity data along with its location second by second as it climbs through the atmosphere." Kalani was brimming with excitement. It was cold in the garage, and his breath froze in clouds as he spoke.

Johnson played along. "How long will that take?"

"About two hours. Then when it gets about twenty-five miles up, the low air pressure causes the balloon to burst, and this parachute"—Kalani pointed again—"drops the radiosonde back down through the atmosphere, taking readings as it goes. Add its readings to the eight hundred that are released at the exact same time throughout the world…" Kalani was getting carried away with the prospect. "And voila! You've got enough data to build a weather model."

Johnson seemed a skeptical. "Eight hundred for the whole world? That doesn't seem like so many."

Kalani's face clouded. "You're right. If I had my way, we'd release eight thousand balloons. Think of the exponential increase in data and accuracy! No more whining about bad forecasts and unexpected weather. But typical government—no one wants to spend money where it really belongs, just waste, waste, waste on other boondoggles."

"So how many balloons are released in South Dakota?"

"Two. Just here and in Rapid City." Kalani delivered the horrible news with a certain relish.

"That's it?"

"Write your congressman." Kalani was somewhat serious. You never knew what a letter from another source could do.

"So when do these get released?"

"Oh-one-hundred Coordinated Universal Time, and twelve hundred UTC—or six o'clock a.m. and p.m. our time, or"—the meteorologist checked his Timex—"in ten minutes."

"Isn't it kinda windy?"

"Tell me about it. About forty miles an hour, gusts to fifty, out of the northwest. There's a big winter cold front coming through. I'd be curious to see where this radiosonde winds up. Anyway, it's gonna be a little tricky. When I give the sign, open the garage door and stand back."

Kalani stood by the helium tank and filled the balloon to about six feet then grabbed near the neck with a gloved hand. Warily, like a bull rider signaling for the bell, he nodded to the high schooler, who raised the garage door.

Instantly, the garage was full of wind and sound. The balloon started whapping back and forth like a speed bag at a gym. Kalani had to shout to be heard. "Is it open all the way?"

It wasn't, and Johnson tried to say so, but it was too late. The balloon leapt out of Kalani's hand and bounded around the garage furiously. The high schooler tried to help herd it outside and managed to push it into a sideways wind that ripped the balloon out and away, yanking the cord with the parachute and the radiosonde with it.

With a jerk, the parachute was caught up in the workings of the garage door, making immediate ripping noises. With shouts of alarm, Kalani ran to help Johnson free the balloon while it twisted around and around at the end of its cord, bouncing against the gravel drive. In a matter of a few extremely long seconds, the balloon was released from its tether and was soon dragging its mangled chute and radiosonde behind it.

"Is that hard on the radio dealie?" Johnson's hands were already red, and his face was pinched against the wind.

As Johnson spoke the words, Kalani saw the balloon bounding along the gravel drive, desperately trying to gain altitude. It looked like it was going to make it, to finally do its meteorological duty, when the radiosonde hit midway through a barbwire fence and whipped around it, binding it tight. Just as fast, the balloon bounded down and started hitting its rubbery beige face against a steel fence post.

Even while running toward it, Kalani could see it wilt and sag into the fence. "Uh-oh."

The two stood there, freezing, in the prestorm wind.

Johnson tried to console Kalani. "Maybe they won't need this one, you know, for the weather stuff."

Kalani looked at him.

Johnson looked back as if trying to think of the right way to say it. "So, uh, do I still get extra credit?"

Chapter 45 - Stacey

Stacey felt a sense of... what was the word? Clarity. Whatever happened that day was supposed to happen. He shrugged mentally. Nothing seemed to disturb his relaxed sense of peace. The smell of the fire still clung to his clothing like incense and offered the same surreal feeling of release. With a detached air, he pulled the Dodge around and headed back toward the Catholic church and the promise he had made to Monty Cooper about checking things out.

He shook his head bemusedly. *What's wrong with you today?* He checked the clock at the bank. Almost a quarter to nine. He was late, a full hour and a half off his normal routine, but he just didn't seem to care. The Dodge stood at the corner stop sign, waiting for Stacey to decide. Left, home. Right, church. It'd be just as easy to drive to the church, ask the priest for answers, then go back home for a shower and shave on the way into the office to pack what little was left. Snowflakes were starting to fall, whipped around by the ever-present wind. The forecast hadn't sounded so bad, but this looked a little more ominous than they had reported. Typical. The sullen gray sky made him think worse weather was on the way.

That sealed it. Better to get the meeting over with before the snow piled up. It would just be a quick couple of questions. Then he'd leave some notes for Darren to follow up on and be done with the whole thing.

It shouldn't take too long.

Chapter 46 - Ippy

One of the reasons women didn't run the world, Ippy decided, was because of poor footwear. She was sitting at her desk, looking out the window and rubbing some life back into her feet. The cause of her pain and suffering lay in a puddle of melting snow by the portable heater at the door. Two fashionably cute winter boots lay in shame, having failed to keep her feet either warm or dry.

It was her own fault, she knew. She had specifically gone to the Campbells Farm and Ranch to get some practical boots for the winter, but next door to Campbells was Drapers with a big SALE sign and these boots in the window that looked fabulous on her and were only half a size too small but were sixty percent off, so she put on thinner socks so they wouldn't chafe so much, and here she was, rubbing her feet, looking out at the weather, and feeling morose.

The wind was easy to see. Clothed in bits of sand, chaff, and occasional pellets of snow, it howled down

the street and made a loose pane of glass at the front of
the radio station chatter randomly. She adjusted her view
to look at the flag above the post office. It was holding
on to its tethered line, mute in the distance. She could
imagine the racket it was making. A good four inches
had already frayed off its end, and it looked to be about
half an hour away from being a square instead of a
rectangle. It was not that cold, somewhere below
freezing, but the overcast sky and the sound of the wind
made a shiver run down her spine.

Now what do I do? She looked around for a cup of
coffee that wasn't the poor excuse for coffee offered to
KDAN employees. While she was at it, she looked for a
fireplace, a good book, and a comforter. And a muffin.
Blueberry.

There was no fireplace at the café, but if she walked
three blocks, she could at least have the coffee and
muffin. Her newscasts had all been recorded onto seven-
minute carts and delivered to the studio. She'd done
enough to last through the noon show and was free to
gather what news she could until the early-morning news
at 6:05 the next morning.

She had a little bit of free time if she wanted to take
it.

Maybe he'll be there. She avoided his name—a way
to deny her attraction to this unlikely man. She had seen
him around town since the election. Once, while walking
around a street corner, she had accidentally bumped into
him. Her mind had been elsewhere, and all of a sudden,
there she was, colliding into him. He was equally
surprised, grabbing her by the shoulders to keep her

from falling, looking down at her with those mournful eyes.

"S-Sorry," she said with no real attempt to move, noticing the way he smelled and the way his hands held her, a small smile underneath his mournful mustache.

"You okay?"

She nodded.

He released her carefully then touched the brim of his hat, like Gary Cooper in one of those old western movies. He'd stepped back, opened his mouth to say something, then closed it again, nodded, taken a small step to the side, and gone on his way.

And now he was in her dreams—stupid, random dreams where they would be sitting watching the sun rise or set, or else just driving along in his old pickup, watching the fields go by. Nothing really happened in those dreams, but whenever she had one, she woke up feeling safe and comfortable... and happy.

Well, it was all as stupid as the winter boots she'd bought. They looked good and seemed as if they might work, but at the end of the day, they were a bad mistake and a waste of time and money. In fact, the whole town—the whole career—seemed like a bad idea. Never had she really thought about it before. It all made sense at Brown. You got a job, you moved from place to place, you got better, and you eventually had a pretty good job doing important things. Lately, she wondered if it was less about what you did and more about who you did it with. She glanced back into the KDAN studios in time to catch Larry Karl leering at her backside. He shrugged through the window and kept leering. Ugh.

She pulled on her still-damp socks and reached for the bad boots. Both seemed to symbolize her situation. She pulled on her gray wool coat—old and substantial, a two-dollar purchase from the thrift store that smelled faintly of mothballs—and stepped out into the weather. *Whoa.* Not bad now, traveling with the wind, but it will be trouble heading back. Maybe it will die down.

Stumbling a bit like a little kid being shoved along by an impatient parent, Ippy groped for her mittens and hat, pulling them on as she walked. Puffs of steam whipped away with each breath. With a wry smile, Ippy picked up the pace. If this was what winter was like, the mothball smell should be blown off her coat by Thanksgiving.

The five-minute walk put color in her cheeks and refroze her feet. By the time she got to the café, she was glad to push her way past the steam-covered glass door and into the warm cloud of food smells, coffee, bread, bacon. She welcomed the mumble of the people gathered there—the Dansing faithful, eating impossibly large caramel rolls and drinking coffee—the clattering of dishes and utensils, and the sound of the never-ending dice game at the table in the back.

As usual, all sound stopped when she walked in. People turned and gazed like curious livestock. Most dismissed her, but a few switched their conversations over to talk about her. Nothing malicious, mainly—she was just new, and new things got talked about. Over a lifetime of moving, she had gotten used to it.

Doris, the broad and efficient woman who ran the café, saw her come in and, without a word, had a cup of steaming coffee on the counter along with a plate and silverware. Doris nodded for her to sit down, so Ippy sidled up to a seat at the counter, sandwiched between a rancher and a mechanic.

"Any rolls left?" The smell of caramel rolls changed her mind away from the muffins.

"Couple." Doris made a few pans of caramel rolls each morning, and when they were gone, they were gone.

Out it came, tall and gooey, lapping over all sides of the small plate it was served on, dribbling caramel onto the Formica countertop. Diets were frowned upon in Doris's café. A large swipe of butter was already melting into the top of the roll, a small lake of decadence.

The place was busy but not packed. Doris was a great cook, and most of the town found a way to spend time there at least a couple times a week. Ippy cut a chunk out of the roll with a fork—it was too big to pick up and eat—and took a bite. Heaven. She then took a sip of the coffee, a strange-tasting brew whose flavor Ippy learned came not from the coffee beans but from the distinctly bad-tasting Dansing water.

Still, it was hot and welcome on a cold day. Two bites in, she glanced up at the mirror along the back of the counter and looked at the crowd.

"He's not here."

Ippy's face flushed a bit. "Excuse me?"

Doris's look was impassive. "The sheriff. Waltraub. He ain't here."

Reddened face aside, Ippy tried to look indifferent. "I'm not interested in the sheriff."

Doris gave her an appraising look then shrugged. "You should be." Then she left to wait on some other customers.

The rancher next to her was obviously eavesdropping. He snickered into his plate of pancakes.

Ippy went back to her eating and pretended it was all a misunderstanding and that she had no intention of accidentally running into him.

Stupid dreams. The last dream had involved a tall woman and a suitcase. Ippy was sitting at a kitchen table, and although she did not recognize the woman, something about her made the conversation warm and familiar, like she was an old friend. The smell of fresh-cut grass blew through an open window. On top of a refrigerator, a small radio played jazz music. Everything about the dream seemed unusually vivid. The colors and smells were bright and clean. Abruptly, the woman pointed to a suitcase and said, "It's time to go."

She had woken then, vaguely disturbed, and even though Stacey Waltraub was not in the dream, it still seemed to be about him.

There was a third of the caramel roll left, and Ippy realized with some dismay that she was going to eat all of it. The rancher was on his feet and pulling his coat on. It wasn't his business, but he chimed in anyway in case she was interested.

"I was a friend of the sheriff before Waltraub, Virg was his name. He was a good one, and Stace was a lot like him. Still feel bad about it. Almost told him so today when I saw him out by the Catholic cemetery—think he was looking for Father Andrew, the new priest."

He was speaking to his empty plate while he dug for some pocket change and a tip. Ippy was tempted to say something smart back, but she said nothing, sipping from her coffee instead.

Three minutes later, she had paid for her roll and coffee and bundled up. As she headed outside, she turned back into the wind and walked about four more blocks to the cemetery. Stupid, she knew, but she was going to go there anyway.

Chapter 47 - Geist

That day, his name was Miller. He was an independent insurance adjuster, and he needed to get to Dansing, South Dakota, to do an estimate on a collapsed building. He spoke in a vague mumble. The trooper at the interstate entrance ramp outside of Rapid City was not focused on him but on the two or three cars behind him that were also looking to get on I-90.

"Sorry, sir, we're closing it down. We got four inches already, and it's just started, and look at it whip across th—hey!"

The four-wheeler behind him was trying to inch around to the right. The trooper was wearing a parka and maroon Mountie hat. His gray mustache was clipped and short, his ears an angry red in the fierce wind.

Staying at Miller's window but shouting across the hood into the driver's window of the other vehicle, the trooper was tired of messing around. "Sir, this interstate is *closed down*. There will *not* be anyone accessing it until further notice." He barked the words like a drill sergeant. He probably had been one back in the day.

Miller looked at the barrier across the ramp. It could be driven through, but not easily. It could also be driven around, but not with the trooper standing there. Miller's finger was on the trigger of the gun in his lap underneath his coat. Two rounds should do it, and in the storm, it would be easy to get away.

The other driver must have complained.

"This is *not* unnecessary! Sir, I have three times gone on searches for drivers who have illegally crossed a barrier. All were stuck. The first were fined ten thousand dollars. One spent an additional twenty days in jail. The third was dead, frozen in the median. This is *not* a joke, sir. This is your *life*!"

Miller studied him and decided he was telling the truth. He also decided that taking any other road would be just as difficult if not more so.

He eased his finger off the trigger. "Officer?" His voice was mild and polite. "I have some business in Dansing. Can you tell me if the roads are blocked there as well?"

"Ninety is blocked clear to Mitchell, and I wouldn't be surprised if that closes by tonight. Last I heard, north to Belle Fourche and over to Timber Lake, it's even worse. Only a fool would go out in this storm."

Miller watched him carefully and again believed him. That meant that the gold was not going anywhere either.

There is no hurry. Any anxiousness on his part was based more on greed than on a real threat. Once the storm cleared, he would have time to find the Catholic church and the people who could be persuaded to help him. He closed his eyes and visualized the map of South Dakota—Sioux Falls on the east, Rapid City on the west, and the concrete ribbon of interstate connecting the two. West of the capitol, Pierre, the town of Dansing was stranded all by itself, ninety miles north of the interstate and completely dependent on clear roads and no wind.

Satisfied, he put the car in reverse and carefully backed off the ramp, following the other cars back into Rapid City and a night or two in a hotel. He gave the handgun a reassuring pat.

Everything was fine.

Chapter 48 - Stacey

What the hell? Twenty-four years, and he still was amazed by the weather. He had figured on a bad winter storm, but the massive Power Wagon was rocking in the wind, its springs creaking above the engine noise. He eased the truck alongside the Catholic cemetery and threw it into park. The wind moaned and whistled around the cab, and a trickle of snow was sifting across the dash even while he sat there.

It was daytime but dark enough to see that there were no lights on in the church or rectory. He was thinking about walking to make sure, but it was a long walk in this weather, and he would pay for each step. *Where the heck is he?*

The cab shook, and the sound of the wind made him shiver involuntarily. Then he looked at the shed, the one that cemetery workers used. There was a light on back there. That would be more of a walk than to the church, but maybe Herman Deuxcamps would know something. Stacey took a breath and opened the door of the truck.

He gripped the handle hard but felt the wind rip at it. Pellets of snow pelted against his coat.

He sighed and stepped out of the cab into snow that drifted to boot height. *Oh well. Part of the job.* Body tense with the cold, Stacey stepped across through the snow toward the shed. Fortunately it wouldn't take very long.

Chapter 49 - Ippy

What the hell? It was cold walking to the café, but this was ridiculous. Feet stiff and numb, she stumbled ahead through snow that was piling up everywhere. Bad enough downtown, it got worse as she headed down the side streets, and now that she could see glimpses of prairie, she could only imagine what it must be like in the open.

Pulling her coat tighter around her, she squinted through the driving snow. A gust pushed her back like a bully on the playground. *Unbelievable*. It was a stupid idea anyway, and she was weighing what the better move would be—going on or turning around—when she saw the sheriff's truck parked up ahead. Pushing forward, she reached it and could see boot tracks, mostly filled with snow, heading into the cemetery. She took a breath, adjusted her scarf around her head, and pressed onward to warmth and shelter.

Chapter 50 - Darren White

People think cops are stupid. No matter what, where, who, or when, people just think we're a little bit on the slow side.

He'd seen it in the military when officers thought he was stupid because they were older and outranked him. He saw it in Sioux Falls when crooks from Chicago thought he was stupid because he was a cop in South Dakota, and he'd seen it again the previous day when Herman Deuxcamps thought he was too stupid to think that something strange was going on. Just because Waltraub was stupid did not mean that he was.

It was the way the Indian looked when he had handed him the other plat book—something about his eyes, the way they shifted a bit—that made Darren curious enough to ignore the storm warnings and wait out in his pickup just to see what Herman was up to.

He waited about two hours. Then, deciding that the time was ripe, he sidled up to the shed in the back of the Catholic cemetery. He could see a light through a window by the garage door. The wind was howling, so there was no chance of being heard, but caution made him move slowly. He tried the door handle. Locked.

He raised an eyebrow. No one locked anything in Dansing. It was the one way to recognize an out-of-towner. Even after the murders that had happened in April of that year, people had a habit of leaving keys in ignitions and doors unlocked.

Hunching his shoulders against the cold, Darren stepped a few feet back and examined the door and his situation. Sturdy door. Cheap lock. Breaking and entering. He stepped back to the window where the light was. It was frosted over. Snow whirled around the glass, making it even harder to see inside.

Leaning in with his ears close, he tried to hear what was going on in the building. It was too windy—not quite a tornado but windy enough you'd need to shout to anyone farther than four feet away.

He walked back to where the door was, his ears red and painful in the cold, snow collecting around the collar of his jacket, making his neck raw with cold.

He looked at the lock and reached inside his coat for the gun in his shoulder holster. A few years back, in Sioux Falls, his partner had tried the same trick, kicking in a similar-looking door. That door was owned by a paranoid recluse who had welded a half-inch steel-plate reinforcement around the door, which had shattered the heel of his partner on impact, earning him several months of painful rehab, a permanent disability, and the nickname Buster.

Hell with it. He took two strong strides and, raising

his right foot, he struck at the door just above the knob with his right heel. *Bang.*

The door flew open on impact, the wood splintering easily. Using the noise and surprise as a distraction, Darren stepped through briskly, drawing his weapon and looking for resistance.

And there was Herman down low, standing in a hole in the ground up to his waist, a surprised look on his face. "What the hell is going on?"

It was a good question. After all, Darren was only working on a hunch, and a split second after entry, it looked to him as if he'd just busted into a church garage, interrupting a gravedigger at work.

Darren decided to go with the bluff. "You know, Herman. You know exactly what's going on."

Herman stared at him for a solid five seconds. Then, shoulder slumping a little, he leaned back against the side of the grave and half sobbed, "God Almighty, I'm so tired."

Darren moved to his right to get a better bead on the Indian and to see if he could detect exactly what was happening. On further inspection, he could see Herman was actually standing about waist-high in a concrete box sunk a good foot in the ground. A concrete lid was propped open alongside the hole, a pry bar by its side. It appeared to be one of those heavy concrete boxes that you sealed caskets in before they were buried.

"Is that a grave?"

Herman looked up at him and shrugged. "Don't think so."

Darren kept his poker face and waited.

Herman continued. "The fake priest was looking for it out in the cemetery—that's why we dug out there. It was only until you brought that other plat book by that I remembered that this shed was built about thirty years ago. I never thought it was built on top of graves, but when I checked, I found there was two graves marked Heiliger—German names—so I thought it was worth a shot.

Darren played along. "Well, whaddya know." Then he guessed a bit. "Did you find them?"

"Them? You mean the bars?"

Bars? "Yeah. The bars."

"I found eight. Heavy suckers. The rest must be right here." Herman nodded to the ground next to the hole.

Darren fished in his pocket and tossed Herman a lighter. Then he gestured with the barrel of his gun. "Show me."

Herman heaved a sigh of exhaustion and relief and resignation. He flicked the lighter and held it low, and Darren could see the glimmer of… his eyes widened.

"Those are bars of gold?"

Herman's eyes narrowed. "Didn't you know?"

Darren shrugged. "I knew it was valuable. I didn't know what it was, though." He took another stab at it. "What did you do with the bodies?"

Herman rubbed his face, sighed again, and fished a cigarette out of his pocket as Darren watched him carefully, waiting.

"Buried 'em. That son of a bitch with the blotched face, he tried to shoot me. Then that fake priest took him out and started after me. It was self-defense, I swear."

Herman became more animated. As he gestured with his hand that held the lighter, the flame blew back, scalding his hand. "Ouch!"

It was an old trick, and Darren was ready for it, eyes not distracted by the flame but looking for the other hand, seeing it come up and out of the dark. He fired instinctively, and the flame of the gunfire illuminated the scene. The Indian cried out in pain as the gun shot out of his hand. It was one shot in a million, a shot that Darren hadn't planned but just did as a defensive reaction.

The smell of cordite mixed with the ringing in Darren's ears. He took a step back, shielding his body behind the tractor. "You done?"

The question reached the Indian, who was holding one hand with the other, nursing it, the lit cigarette still hanging off the end of his lips. He slumped a little. "Yeah." He took a drag and sighed it out. "You tell Stacey?"

Darren was looking at the gold in the bottom of the grave. Eyes adjusted, he could now make out some details. Were those swastikas stamped in the tops of the bars?

"How many bars are there?"

"That blotch-faced bastard said there was a couple hundred pounds, but I figured he was lying. The plat map has four graves marked, so I figure thirty-two bars."

Holy. Shit.

A gust of wind sent the door flapping against the wall, making both men jump.

"You gonna arrest me?"

Darren knelt down and considered his options. He

had no handcuffs. It was snowing something terrible, a full-on blizzard. He was not yet officially sheriff, so he'd need to make a citizen's arrest, something he had never done before, and he was uncertain on the correct procedure.

"No." He shot Herman in the body once and then in the head twice, just to be sure.

Chapter 51 - Ippy

Her feet were numb, as were her ears and face. The snow seemed to come from everywhere, matting into her hair and around her neck. She could see things but not very clearly, shapes only, and even they would disappear in the maelstrom of driving snow. She had heard of blizzards, had been caught in some pretty bad weather, but never had she been out in a storm like this.

She knocked on the door of the rectory first, standing on its broad porch, semisheltered from the worst of the wind, hopping from one foot to the other, trying to avoid freezing, the pounding of her fists muted in her gloved hand. The dark, empty interior ignored her.

Pacing back and forth, she tried peering into the curtained depths, shouting an inquiry, pressing on the doorbell. The smashed-in button gave her no encouragement.

She looked down at her cute boots and cursed them. It seemed silly to die on a front porch and even sillier to smash her way into the house of a priest. *Maybe he's in back.* Stumbling on numb feet, she slipped her way across the broad cement porch and down the steps, deciding to circle around to the back.

Choosing the least windy route, she waded through the swirls of snow and found herself looking at a back door that was just as locked and just as deserted as the front. *Screw it.* No man needed to be followed, no matter how pathetic. Stepping off the back step, she did a quick check of the surroundings. A momentary gap in the swirl of flakes showed what looked like a shed or garage or something. In that brief glimpse, she saw two things that interested her. The first was a light shining from a window, and the second was a plume of smoke coming from its chimney.

Heat.

Pulling her snow-matted scarf up around her eyes, she struck out for the shed. Two steps later, she heard what sounded like… a gunshot? She stopped in the snow, puzzled, not sure what she had heard in the wind. Then came one, two, three shots—definitely shots. That meant someone was in trouble. She started running.

Chapter 52- Stacey

Stacey was leaning into the wind, high-stepping through the snow and watching out for tombstones, which were hard to make out in the full onslaught of blinding flakes, when he heard a shot. He instinctively grabbed for the sidepiece that was not with him. *Stupid. Stupid, stupid stupid.* He kept a varmint gun in the rack of the Power Wagon, a twenty-two rifle over a 440 shotgun.

He was halfway turned back to the truck when he heard more shots, three in succession. Bang. Bang-bang! He wheeled back to look, indecisive, and saw the small figure charging for the door through the snow from a different direction. It was only a split second, a flash of dark clothing through a blizzard of white, but he knew with absolute certainty who it was.

It was Ippy.

No.No.No.NO *NO*!! He didn't say the words—they came out as a moan of terror. He charged forward, stumbling ahead like a raging bear, his heart full of fear and foreboding.

Chapter 53 - Darren

"What happened?"

The voice came from the door. Darren jumped and wheeled around. "Shit!"

"Are you okay? I heard gunshots!"

It was the new gal from the radio. Even though she was covered in snow, he recognized her, the one they called the Hawaiian hottie. Her cheeks were red, and her black hair was matted with snow.

He lowered his gun and put it behind his back, instinctively guilty. "He tried to shoot me."

Not focused on him, her eyes were searching around the room for the person he was talking about. "Is he hurt?"

Darren had not thought of this. He had no plan. One second, two seconds of silence passed as he tried to think of a plan. And then it got even worse when another shape came in the broken door, face and mustache caked in white.

"What happened?" It was Waltraub. Shit. Shit. *Shit.*

The woman looked up at Waltraub. "Someone shot at the new sheriff. He looks like he's in shock."

"Where is he?" Waltraub looked around. From where both were standing, neither could see the Indian lying in the bottom of the vault. The lid was propped open, obstructing their view.

Well, it was too bad about the girl—Darren would have liked to make a play with her—but as far as Waltraub went, there was no love lost there. Deciding, Darren motioned to the bottom of the vault and acted shocked. "H-He tried to shoot me. I-I tried to stop…" He let his voice trail off while Waltraub and the girl circled around him to see.

The woman reacted first, jumping into the vault. "He's shot—can't see how bad. We'll need to get him out of here, now." She acted as if she knew what she was doing. She probably had some kind of nurse or medic training.

Waltraub was already kneeling down, getting down into the vault, ready to lift the Indian up.

"Don't bother. He's dead." Darren cocked the gun and pointed. "Just stay down there."

Waltraub paused, frozen. Slowly, he looked up at Darren with a measured gaze. "Better tell me, Darren."

"Nothing really to tell, Stacey. You don't mind if I call you that, do you?" The more Darren thought about it, the better it looked. "That purple-faced fella with the missing finger? Well, he came to Herman down there with some kinda cockamamie story about Nazi gold buried in Dansing. Said that the priest—I knew something was off about that guy—was looking to dig up graves in the cemetery to find some bars of gold."

Darren shook his head as he spoke, still kind of dazed about how it all came together. "'Course, I had no idea about any of this. I just came out here on a hunch that Herman down there was up to something. He tried to shoot me." The lie made him feel better.

"So what're you pointing that at us for?" Waltraub's gaze never left him. His hands were careful, away from his body.

"Not sure exactly. You seem a little dangerous to me, Sheriff… Waltraub." Darren was irritated at the slip. "Seems kinda convenient that you and your little honey should show up like this."

The girl looked daggers at him. "You. Are an ass." She raised her chin. Her lips curled as if she'd tasted something bad. "And a murderer." As she said the word, her expression changed from disdain to horror as she realized she had guessed the right answer.

He tilted his head a bit to the side, a nod to the truth. Darren was thinking. Four shots for the Indian. That left two rounds. If he'd had his 1911 pistol with the clip, it wouldn't be a concern, but a revolver had limitations. He could probably shoot through Waltraub and get two for one, but his time on the force had told him how chancy handgun fire was. Better get them relaxed, calm them down, give them hope for a way out.

"Tell you what, Waltraub. Reach down nice and easy and grab one of those bricks. Put it up here on the dirt."

Bending slowly, eyes never leaving Darren's face, Waltraub reached to pick up a bar. It was still lustrous in the dim light. Waltraub stopped and closed his eyes, shoulders shaking silently. It took Darren a second to figure out what was wrong with the man.

"Are you *laughing*?"

Now the man was laughing out loud, roll upon roll of mirth building upon itself until he started gasping, trying to gain his breath.

"What the hell is so funny?"

"F-F-Fool's gold..." Waltraub was still gasping, eyes slits of merriment, holding the bar in one hand then tossing it into the other. "Man, man, man, that is rich!"

Darren, mad, was tempted to shoot him just to get him to shut up.

Waltraub continued. "You never looked at this, did you? I mean up close? Gold is supposed to be heavy. Sixty pounds a bar anyway. This..." He tossed the bar, hefting its weight. "Hell, I don't know what it is, but it sure as hell ain't gold."

He tossed the bar up easily for Darren to catch.

Darren's eyes focused in on the bar coming easily at him chest high. He reached to palm it with his left hand... and too late realized his mistake. Far heavier than he thought, the bar caught him by surprise, carrying his left hand down and into the edge of the tractor, smashing his fingers against its sharp edges. "Ow!"

Then Waltraub was leaping up with both hands, surprisingly fast, reaching up and up. Reacting, Darren swung the barrel down and leveled a shot. Wide. Waltraub pulled down on top of the vault. The heavy lid was slamming down on Waltraub and the girl. Darren had time for a hasty shot into the shadow where the ex-sheriff was standing. He must have hit him for sure.

Then with the sound of falling concrete, the lid slammed down on the vault, causing the ground to shake.

In the stillness, Darren tried to understand what had just happened. The wind outside was blowing snow in through the open door. He heard the crackle of the fire in the wood stove, the beating of his heart. His left hand throbbed—a sprain or even a break—and it hurt like hell. The realization that he had been fooled, outsmarted by Waltraub, who was now inside a closed vault—all of these thoughts and sensations worked their way into his awareness as the heat of the moment died away.

The two had not escaped. They were trapped. It was over. He'd won. He was alive. He was rich.

The thought gave him a thrill and stirred him to action. *It's not over yet.* Cautiously, he moved to the vault and looked down at it. The lid was heavy, thick concrete, probably five hundred pounds. It had a flange around the edge so it would seal—not long before the air would be used up.

He reached for a shovel and started piling dirt in and around the vault, a couple of shovelfuls, and then he stopped. The pain of his injured hand made handling a shovel awkward.

Wincing, Darren leaned back and thought. He could suck up to the pain and keep shoveling, which would be a good idea if Waltraub was still alive. Let's see him lift three feet of dirt! Or he could leave them there and pull his truck around. That would give them time to suffocate, plus there was extra ammo in the cab.

Just then, a blast of air whirled more snow through the doorway. The storm was getting worse. If he waited too long, he might not be able to move his truck through the drifting snow.

Darren gently flexed his injured hand, which was puffing up around the small finger, and felt a sharp pain. He swore. Probably broke a bone.

The thought of meeting an angry Waltraub with a broken hand made him reach instinctively for his revolver, which was empty. Making his decision, he deposited his gun in his shoulder holster and picked up the bar of gold.

Heavy! It wasn't sixty pounds—that was part of the trick—but heavy anyway. *Fool's gold, my ass.* No way was he going to leave it there. Shifting the bar to his good hand, Darren headed into the maelstrom and toward his truck

Chapter 54 - Ippy

Panic. Stifling, crushing panic pressed down on her, nothing but inky-black absolute nothing. Her face was pressed against a rough, hard surface, and her hand was caught under her body, which was twisted and askew. She wanted, needed to be free, but a heavy, crushing weight pushed down, down, down on top of her.

She took panicky breaths, yet she was still suffocating. She heard a whimpering cry, high-pitched and desperate, a person too afraid to scream. That voice, far removed, was her own, and that made her all the more frightened.

On top of her, a heavy, crushing weight shifted, relieving pain from her shoulders and adding it to her hips and lower back. A heavy groan came from nearby, maybe a foot or so away, but whoever had made it was completely invisible in the palpable pressing blackness.

She needed to breathe but could not get enough air into her lungs. What did come in smelled of blood and urine and feces. She was not sure whose.

Ippy was not claustrophobic, but she was wrapping her mind around what had just happened—the shots, the fall, the heavy lid slamming down into darkness. The helpless feeling added to her panic. She couldn't stop herself from hyperventilating.

Click.

Sudden light. She saw a flickering faintness from off to her left, certainly dim but strong enough to erase complete blindness and help her get a grip on the edge of her fears. She could see the rough texture of the dark concrete. Her right cheek rested on the work boot of the dead Indian.

"Is that a match?" she asked.

"Lighter. Old Zippo I carry in my shirt pocket. You all right?"

Just the sound of his voice knocked more of the fear away.

"Never better." She tried to sound calm, humorous, ironic, like him. "And you?"

"Hard to say. I think I'm shot." It was matter-of-fact, like talking about the weather. *Looks like clouds, rain maybe. I've been shot.*

She decided to match his tone. "Bad?"

A slight groan. "Like I got kicked by a horse. Something's wrong with my belly. It's starting to burn."

"That's not good."

"Nope."

"You know what exactly happened?"

"Darren started shooting. I pulled the lid down on the vault to stop the bullets. Seemed like a good idea at the time."

"I don't suppose you could get your fat ass off of me?"

She felt a shifting of weight and heard a soft, gasping groan.

"That better?"

"Not much," she said.

"Hold on a sec." The light went out. "Here's the deal. I gotta shift around onto my back and see if I can push this lid off. I can't keep this thing lit while I do it. You're gonna have to figure a way to get out from under me, get me a clear space to work. You ready?"

It was better to think of a task than the horrible possibility. "Yes." Click. The light flickered. Ippy saw how she could shift a little, scoot, and rotate to the side. "Okay. I'm ready."

The light went out. Squirming and shifting, she made it onto her side with her back to the concrete. The light flicked on again, and she could see the profile of Stacey, lying on his back, his knees near the top of her head. Underneath him was the inert body of the groundskeeper, mostly hidden from view. His head appeared to be trapped under the small of Stacey's back.

A dark stain was covering the front of Stacey's coat. Ippy reached for it, and her hand came away sticky.

"You're bleeding!"

"Not surprised."

"Can you shift the lid?"

Stacey moved his legs and moaned. "Not yet. I'll need more room and some help with my legs. Can you shift Herman out from under me?"

"Lemme see." The light flickered. "Yeah, maybe.

Scoot as far over as you can, and I'll try moving his feet first, then his hips, and so on. Okay?" The light flicked off in assent.

Gasping and struggling, Ippy groped in the dark, tugging and pulling the dead body over inch by inch. "Light, please."

Click.

The body's lower half had shifted, the top still stuck under Stacey. The flame was weaker, more yellow. She didn't want to think about what that meant.

Stacey's voice was grim. "Screw it. We'll go with what we got. My stomach muscles musta got hit somehow. On the count of three, you're gonna hafta help me lift my feet up and brace them on the lid."

Ippy reached and grabbed his right knee. Her leverage was wrong for lifting, but there was nothing to do about it. On three, Stacey moaned and lifted his right knee up, kicking his boot out to brace against the lid. The light went out. In the dark, Ippy could hear the moan and a second boot scraping against the heavy concrete lid.

Again, there was a flick of the light, feebler than before. Stacey's face glistened with sweat. He glanced down and tried a smile. "Okay, let's do this. Find something to shim under the lid once I lift it." Ippy looked around.

"There's some gold bars."

He gave a rough laugh. "Well, if you can lift it, fine. Let me know when you're ready."

Ippy could raise herself to not quite sitting. Bracing on her elbow, she grabbed a bar. *God Almighty, it's heavy!* She shifted it to her stomach. "Okay."

The light went out.

In the dark, she heard a deep breath. Then another. Then a quiet moan of exertion. The moan continued, turned deeper, then became a growl of pain and focus.

She saw a dim light and cracks of visibility and felt a rush of cool air. The lid rose one inch, two—a final grunt, and four inches of vault lid opened by Ippy's head. With a grunt, she curled and pressed up with the bar, seeking to wedge it in place. There!

"Got it!"

A sigh and groan followed as the lid lowered down on the bar. Then came a space of silence and a wry comment. "Well, he can shoot us now."

"Can you shift around and get to the other end?"

A pause. "No." Then there was another pause. "I think you can do it, though."

"Me?"

"How tall are you?"

"Five-five."

"That should be about right. If you can work your way up here to the other end, you can stand with your feet on the floor and bend over, lift the whole thing with your legs and hips." His voice was shaking with fatigue.

Ippy doubted she could do it but knew she needed to try. She wriggled over on top of him and shimmied her way up his body till she was even with him, eye to eye. His face was pale, shiny with sweat and fatigue.

"Are you okay, Stace?"

She caught a corner of a smile beneath that forlorn mustache. "You kiddin'? I been dreaming of this." He raised one eyebrow.

Men.

Shimmying farther, she reached the other end of the vault and crouched on hands and knees, looking down at his face upside down. "Like this?"

Again came the small smile. "Your blouse is untucked."

She flushed a bit despite the predicament. "Don't get any ideas, cowboy."

On her feet, bent completely over with hands on knees, she pressed her rump against the lid.

"Now exhale, and extend your legs, pushing away down through your heels."

"It's too heavy."

"Nope. Not for you. Women are just as strong in the legs as men. Exhale and push through, and let your legs do all the work." She nodded at him, braced herself, and pushed. Nothing.

"Give it all you got. Get mad and shove through it."

She tried again, angry at her own weakness and the thought of Darren getting away with it.

There! She felt a small shift, then a lifting and hovering as the whole end of the lid balanced on the small of her back.

"Shift the whole thing over and to the right."

She did that and felt the lid teetering on three points of contact.

"Keep shifting it."

As he said it, the lid tilted suddenly and fell partially off to the side. A long triangular opening as wide as eight inches appeared. A slice of light showed his pale face and a patch of blood, wet and shiny, across his stomach.

His voice was level and matter-of-fact. "Well, you might as well squeeze through and get that pry bar by the tractor. We've got some work to do before Darren gets back."

Chapter 55 - Greta

The sod house that Greta lived in was made for bad weather like this. The walls were a good two feet thick, plus there was the fence pounded out ten feet around the house's perimeter, trapping any blowing snow and forming a deep drift of insulation all around the house.

Jimmy had taught her all of the tricks of wintering through the plains before he died, and she was at least as comfortable in winter as in any other season.

The wood stove was also the cookstove. A Dutch oven with baked beans in it was adding its aroma to the dim surroundings. Jimmy had always sworn by Kentucky pole beans, so every year, Greta would plant a couple rows and water them through the growing season, letting them dry down in the pods then shucking them into old mayonnaise jars. All winter, her evening meal would consist of baked beans.

Greta took a serving off the top and put it on a chipped plate to cool. While it sat, Greta added a cup of beans back into the Dutch oven along with a little water, brown sugar, and spices, then stirred it up and put the lid back on. The next night, she would repeat the process. Theoretically, some of those beans would cook for five months straight.

Reaching into an old Coke slide cooler, she fished out a bottle of beer and sat down to eat at the small Formica table. The other place was set for Jimmy. Sometimes he came, and sometimes he didn't. Maybe he was home. She glanced at the small box on the shelf and wondered.

Oh, good. Beans.

Jimmy. He had a way about him, showing up at the most unpredictable times.

Her heart gave a little leap just like it always did when he was around. Her answer was gruff. "Laugh, clown, laugh. You gonna sit or talk?"

He said nothing. That usually meant trouble of some kind. Sighing with frustration, she plunked her fork down.

"Oh great. What is it?"

Gonna need a little help is all.

"What now? It's a blizzard out there!"

You've been in blizzards before.

"Yeah, they're dangerous, miserable things, which is why I'm here, warm and safe inside, eating my supper and not going anywhere."

She shifted her chair with a huff, turning away from the table, glowering at the cookstove. She ate several mouthfuls in silence, pretending it was delicious. When the silence got heavy, she got up and turned on the radio. She lived next to the Dansing radio tower—it was on her property—so KDAN was the only station she listened to. KDAN was the only station she *could* listen to since it drowned out all others.

It was that horse's ass, Larry Karl, reading business and school closings and pontificating about the serious nature of the storm. She made it about four long minutes.

"Satan in a swimsuit!" She got up and shut it off with a vicious twist of the knob and glared at Jimmy. "What the hell is it?"

It's a walk... probably two miles total. Not terrible cold, but you'll want to dress for the wind and the wet. I'll guide you.

"Typical. No answering my questions, just showing up when you feel like it, telling me what to do, and no details."

Jimmy paid no attention. His focus was on the storm. Better hurry, darlin'.

Chapter 56 - Stacey

On the whole, Stacey thought, it could have been a lot
worse. The pain was like a hot poker searing across his
middle. Ippy had him down on a piece of plywood. She
told him to lie still. She must've had some training in
nursing, since she moved with a gentle efficiency,
working with a first aid kit that must have been
somewhere in the shed. The pain was bad, but the touch
of her hand was cool and calming like a healing balm.
They were still in danger, but Stacey had a hard time
focusing on what needed to be done and was instead lost
in the intimate touch of her fingers.

"Well, it's a mess but just a surface wound. You got
one bullet that ricocheted off your belt buckle, up and
across your belly—a nasty furrow, but deep as it is, it
did not go into your abdominal cavity." She glanced up
at him. "You have some thick abdominal muscles."

"So I've been told." Stacey winced against a wave of
pain. "I had an emergency appendectomy about ten years
ago. The surgeon in Rapid City hung around the

recovery room to wait until I woke up. Guess he was curious. Said I had a wall of stomach muscle an inch and three quarters deep. He wondered what I did for a living." He winced again.

"Well, it's thick but not bulletproof. There's a lot of meat that's tore up here. The bleeding is serious but not bad, all capillary. I can pack it until we get an ambulance here."

"I think you better be a little more aggressive." Stacey nodded to the door, still open with the cold air pushing snow into the shed. "I got a bad feeling about that door, and I think time is running out. I think you should do what you can to patch this up."

Ippy frowned. "Well, that dead groundskeeper must have been a medic or something back in the day—either that, or he's been preparing for the Apocalypse. The medical kit is army-surplus field-hospital stuff, even has sulfa powder and morphine hypos, which are probably illegal and probably outdated. But"—she looked over her shoulder at the door with the plywood blocking it—"I can try."

Stacey nodded. Ippy shrugged and opened a pack of rubber gloves that looked too thick to be anything close to new. Then she dumped some rubbing alcohol on the gloves, opened a packet with a syringe, and shot a little jet of clear liquid into the air. She proceeded to stab little shots of the liquid into the oozing groove in his belly.

He felt lightheaded and cold and decided he didn't need to see any more.

"Yeah, I wouldn't look either."

The burning pain was already subsiding, so he

decided to look at her eyes only, watching them
concentrate as she opened packets of sterile pads and
cleansers and threaded something that looked like a fish
hook. He felt a tugging in and around his belly as if
someone were mending his shirt while he was still
wearing it.

There was a pleasant sound that it took a while for
him to recognize. She was humming—a quiet, tuneless
humming that was part whisper, part lullaby. Very
soothing.

"It will take a few more minutes. I'm just trying to
sew the meat together on the inside as best I can, nothing
pretty, then I'll suture up the skin and wrap you like a
Christmas turkey. You probably oughta have a real
doctor check it out, or you might wanna save some
money and heal on this. I work cheap, and if it doesn't
get infected, you'll have a story to tell your kids and
grandkids."

"Kids." The way he repeated the word made her
blush a little and look flustered.

"Sorry," she said.

"It's okay." He wondered if she had any children but
changed the subject instead of asking about it. "You do
this pretty well. You work in a hospital ever?"

"You might say so." She had a hint of a twinkle in
her eye. "Thought I might try medicine when I was
younger, before I joined the army, so I interned for a
while at a country practice. He said I had potential."

"He let you do this kind of work?"

"Yeah. There weren't too many laws about it, and
the farmers didn't seem to mind."

"Farmers?"

"Yeah. He was a vet." She patted his shoulder and smiled wide, showing dimples and perfect white teeth. "Large animal."

Chapter 57 - Darren

The storm was worse, white clots of snow blasting sideways, stinging exposed flesh, lowering visibility to near zero. He staggered to his truck, climbed in, and slammed the cab closed. A dust of flakes covered the dash from where they had filtered through the vents. His breath came out as steam and fogged the windshield.

He swore at the cold as he clawed off his gloves and put the key in the ignition. The engine roared to life, and even though it would take a while for the heater to work, Darren set the defrost blower to high.

The cab rocked in the wind. The howling was louder than the blower. Visibility was better now that he didn't have to squint against the snow. The sky was turning dark, and a house light could be seen.

He looked at the bar of gold on the passenger seat and touched its hard, cold surface reverently. *I am rich.*

He looked back through the truck window toward the cemetery shed. Nothing had changed. Having a loaded gun seemed unnecessary. They were probably dead or would be shortly. The more he thought about it, the more certain he was that he had shot Waltraub and that the sheriff and the girl had suffocated. The fact that Darren had a gun that tied him to a dead man—that seemed more worrisome.

He needed to think. As long as there was a blizzard, no one would be traveling. He had time to act, to clean things up, but he needed to do the right things in the right way in the right order.

First thing, ditch the gun. Later, he could claim he lost it in the blizzard. Next, go home and get some supplies. Work clothes, garbage bags, food, gloves— these things came to mind, but he would need a list when he got home, to make sure he had everything. Third, drive back to the cemetery and finish getting the gold. No reason he wouldn't have all night to dig up the graves, load the gold into the pickup, and bury all the bodies. It was perfect really. He was the sheriff, looking for missing people. No one would suspect that they would be buried in the cemetery. All the people he would have to worry about were already dead.

"Priest? A fake. He must've run off with the Indian and the guy with the purple face. Waltraub and the girl? Obviously they had a thing for each other, and look at his history—he used to be a carny, for God's sake. No surprise they ran off."

Then he'd hide the gold, lie low for a while, and figure out how he would sell it. That shouldn't be too hard.

Darren drove slowly out of town, keeping his eyes on the road. It was as bad as he had ever seen, definitely whiteout conditions in many spots, but he had experience. The secret was to keep your eye on the fence line or power poles and feel your way along the shoulder, not too fast. He only lived a couple miles out of town, and it was a straight shot. The cab was starting to warm up, and the darkness was creeping in. Darren kept his lights on low beam to get under the driving flakes. High beams only made it worse.

The engine stuttered a little bit, and Darren looked down at the gauges. Not a problem. This truck featured two tanks, and it was a simple matter to switch the gauge to the other pump. With a click, he watched the gauge climb reassuringly to full again. The engine coughed and died. Patiently, he twisted the key. It turned easily enough but without a single cough.

Shit. He knocked on the dash. *Maybe something is loose.* He tried it again. Nothing. Still patient, with the confidence of someone who only bought new vehicles, Darren turned on the dome light and fished the new-smelling owner's manual out of the new-smelling glove box. He found the index and looked up "Trouble Shooting: fuel."

The friendly guide told him that his brand-new truck had two fuel tanks and two fuel pumps, insinuating that that was twice as good as one-tank models. Only later in the manual did it admit that if a fuel pump should malfunction, the best course of action was to switch back over to the other tank and drive to your nearest dealership for four-star, full-warranty service.

Darren sat and let the irony sink in. He had a completely empty tank with a good pump six inches away from a completely full tank with a bad pump.

He swore, more out of anger than out of fear. Those assholes at the dealership in Rapid City had made their last deal with him, by God!

He put on his flashers and looked at the bar of gold. *Shit*. He had a white truck just off the road in a blizzard. What were the odds of it getting hit by someone? And what were the odds of those people then getting out of their vehicle to check on his?

Too risky. Sighing with frustration—this could easily add two more hours to his schedule—he pulled on his gloves, working gingerly over his broken hand, and tugged on his hat. Rethinking his situation, he reached under the seat for his box of cartridges and loaded his revolver, tucking it inside his coat, and cradled the bar of gold in his arms. *Man, this sucker is heavy!*

He headed outside. The good news was that his place was only a half a mile away if he cut across Ned Backer's field.

What a pain in the ass.

Chapter 58- Greta

Greta had been out with Jimmy before in blizzards. She was never afraid when she was with him, just cold. She was small framed, with the body of a twelve-year-old boy, but the joints weren't young. They creaked and complained in the cold weather.

Bundled up, she walked slowly and steadily, one foot in front of the other, pulling a toboggan behind her. Not too fast—the worst thing she could do was work up a sweat. The wind drove against her storm coat, a heavy wool thing with a shorn beaver collar she had gotten at the thrift store. It weighed near as much as she did, but it kept out the wind.

One foot in front of the other. Jimmy could no longer be seen, but that didn't matter. She could feel him.

She was somewhere out by Ned Backer's place when she almost tripped over a lump covered in snow. Stumbling, her knee fell into something soft and yielding. Pulling her scarf away from her eyes to see, she shielded her face with her mittened hand and knelt in the snow. It was a person, mostly buried in snow, almost invisible in the pelting storm.

She fumbled for a small flashlight deep in her coat pocket and wiped the snow away from the face of… the new sheriff!

Her eyes narrowed. "I like the old sheriff better."

I know.

"You are a soft-headed sap and always was one." Working quickly, Greta brushed the snow completely away from Darren's face and knelt, her head down close to his mouth. He was alive.

"You okay, Sheriff?"

Shivering, he said something she could not understand. She felt down his body and legs, and he twitched when she got to his left knee. Even through the mittens, she could feel that it was swollen badly.

Good thing I brought the toboggan. She pulled it around and was reaching to heave the prostrate body onto the sled when she noticed his arms were hugging something. Leaning in, she dusted off the snow. It looked like a brick, although why the hell someone would be carrying a brick in a blizzard was beyond her. *I'll worry about that later.*

Reaching over the sled, she grabbed him by the jacket and rolled him toward her and onto the toboggan. The brick slipped out of his arms and landed next to his body on the sled.

Ahead of her, her tracks heading back to the house had already mostly filled with snow. With a resigned sigh for the work ahead, Greta put her shoulder into the rope and leaned forward.

Chapter 59 - Darren

Darren came to with a start, like waking from a nightmare. The last thing he remembered was falling and twisting his knee and the numbing snow pellets hitting the side of his face. Now here he was, warm, hot almost, next to a wood stove—clothing wet, knee swollen and aching, hand sharp with pain, but alive.

Suddenly, he remembered the gold and reached for it.

"Looking for this?"

It was Greta, the crazy lady who lived out by the radio tower. She was standing in what must have been her house, holding the bar of gold in one hand, elbow braced against her belly and hip jutting out to hold it up.

"You better talk, mister." Her eyes were pale and cold and seemed to peel away layers until she could see what he was trying to hide.

He looked at the stove instead, feeling its heat radiating through his sodden clothes. "Guess you saved my life. I musta passed out."

"You did." The answer was flat. Silence stretched out between them.

Darren took a controlled breath and figured he would start with the truth and see where it took him. "You know we got a new priest in town? Well, he ain't a priest. Near as I can figure, he's a crook who figured out there was some gold hidden away in the church somewhere. I thought something was fishy, but since I'm not the sheriff yet, I mean not officially, I was just going to ask around a bit, see what I could find out. Well, I got to the shed out in back of the church and saw a light on. The snow was starting to pick up, so I just went in, and I saw a pile of these—what looked like bars of gold—and when I stopped to pick one up, this priest guy was behind me and took a swing at me with a shovel. Well, I got my hand up in time to get it broke, then he took a backswing and stove in my ribs."

Darren winced and reached into his coat. "He musta cracked a couple."

The woman's eyes were cold and measuring. "I think you're lyin'. A guy with a shovel who surprises you sure ain't gonna let you pick up a heavy bar of gold and walk out, is he?"

Darren shrugged, pulled out the revolver, flicked loose the safety, and cocked it. "Nope." He pointed it at her stomach. "But it gave me enough time to fish this out. Drop that bar of gold right there."

"Dang it!" She was furious at the trick. "Dang it!" Defiant, she shifted her weight and tossed the heavy bar, not on the ground but at his bad knee.

Bang! The shot rang out, deafening in the confined

room. A red patch of blood blossomed suddenly out of her right thigh, kicking her off her feet and down. The bar of gold landed on its edge on his kneecap, making him see stars.

A keening moan came from across the floor, barely noticed by Darren as he grabbed at his knee. "You bitch!"

The moaning continued. "Jimmy! Jimmy! Let me go, Jimmy! Let me go!"

Darren levered another shot over her head to get her attention. "Shut up!"

Still moaning, grabbing her thigh with both hands, the woman sat up and glared at him. "Well, you fooled Jimmy. I'll give you that. But now you shot me, the only person who can help you, while you're stuck in a blizzard with a bar of gold with a Nazi swastika on it and a lot of explaining to do."

Darren smiled grimly. "And I have a gun, and I'm the sheriff, and I got plenty of time to figure out my new story."

She was sitting on the floor too far away for a good shot. There was a chance she'd get behind an old daybed, maybe make life a little complicated for him. Better to get her closer.

"Get over here in front of the stove."

"You're not going to hurt my Jimmy, are you?"

Jimmy was her husband. Dead and gone well before Darren was born. He shrugged.

She looked sad and pitiful, the starch completely out of her. Now she was just an old and feeble woman, bleeding down one leg, whimpering, with tears streaming down her face and chin trembling. Pathetic.

"Where's Jimmy now?" He felt disdain but also curiosity. The rumors around town about her crazy behavior had made him wonder just what her story was. Better to find out before she was dead.

Tentatively, she reached up over the stove to a cluttered shelf and a wooden box. On the side of it was printed the word "Home."

Wincing, she carefully held the box out in front of her, holding it gently as if it were a beloved child.

"Is that his ashes?"

She lifted a cast-iron lid on top of the stove and tossed the box in. Chin up, she gave him a look of utter disdain. "Nope. It's yours."

A brilliant explosion ripped through the room.

*****

Jimmy had set the box very carefully on the small table. "This here is what we'll use to dig a livestock pond."

Curious, Greta peered down at it. "What is it?"

Jimmy went on explaining in his own sweet time, an aggravation that wore on Greta's patience. "Frienda mine works over on road construction. He showed me this."

Jimmy sat down and smiled, his teeth white and clean in his sunburned face. "Said if you wanna dig a pond, the quick way is you dig a post hole ten, fifteen feet down then fill it with nitrogen fertilizer. Then you pour some fuel oil on top of it, get it good and soaked. Then run like hell."

Greta felt awed. "You light it?"

Jimmy nodded.

"What if it don't go off?"

"Said that could happen. Said the most dangerous thing was to get curious and head back too soon."

"So?" she asked.

"So he gave me these little home sticks." Jimmy opened the box carefully, and Greta could see the dark-red sticks nestled in their bed of shavings.

"Home sticks?"

Jimmy smiled wryly. "Yep. Said if you want to go home and see your maker, these'll get you there in a hurry."

Well, Jimmy had gone home all right, well before the pond was dug. Many a night, Greta had sat by the fire, holding the box, wondering when she might join him.

Week Three

Chapter 60 - Stacey

The blizzard lasted three days. It was impossible to move, so they bolstered themselves against the storm and made the plan.

Stacey's belly was starting to itch, and what wasn't itching hurt like hell. And yet there was more than physical pain—there was a festering in his mind as well. The thought of the gold was a polarizing force that gripped his thoughts and dreams. Too late for them. They are dead, and the crime has been committed. Someone has to find it. Why not you? And what about sunken treasure from pirate ships? Wasn't that in essence the very same thing?

Whenever he thought about it, he felt an increased pressure around his heart, an undeniable weight pressing down.

The sun blazed down with bright cold light, turning everything blinding white. He squinted against the glare, breathing out steam, belly stiff and sore. He heaved up against the side of the Power Ranger, cold sweat chilly against the light breeze.

"I told you not to be lifting anything." Her voice startled him, made him jump a bit. Ippy gave him a curious look as though she could see the argument in his mind. Her hand grasped a burlap sack with a single heavy lump in it. She was walking around the corner of the shed, listing a bit to the side.

"Yeah, yeah." Stacey had gotten out of the cab and, by bracing one hand against the bed of the truck and carefully stooping, was lifting the small pile of burlap sacks one by one into the back of the truck.

"Listen, cowboy. You wanna bust that stitching open?"

Stacey countered, a little snappish. "You wanna stick around and wait for Darren?"

She lifted her chin but didn't say anything.

"This is all of it?"

She nodded.

Three solid days of horrific winds and blowing snow. Three days to dig and discover. Three days to cover their tracks and plan. Darren was bound to show up. The fact that he hadn't was making them both nervous.

Ippy answered his thought. "He's probably stuck somewhere. We got some time probably." Nevertheless, she quickened her pace a bit, helping hoist the last few bags into the back. "At least the extra weight will help with traction."

He nodded then headed to the cab, wincing as he

went.

"You want me to drive to the station?"

"It's a stick."

"I can drive a stick."

He nodded again. She was right. It hurt more than he thought it would, and he needed the rest if they were going to stick to the schedule. Easing into the passenger side of the cab, he tried to hide a gasp. *God almighty, it hurts.*

Ippy hopped in beside him and turned the key. The big block chugged to life. Working the shift lever around, getting a feel for it, Ippy frowned with concentration. "You ready?"

"Yep." The jitters rose up in him. *By God, we are almost home free.* He turned slightly. "You got 'em all, right?"

"All except the one he took. Thirty-one in all."

Just a little nagging doubt, a little distance between them. After all, it was a lot of money. She stopped the truck outside the radio station and got out.

Sighing, he slid over to the driver's seat. "Sure about this?"

"I sure am, cowboy." Looking around carefully, she gave him a hypo. "Jab it in the meat of your thigh if you need it. It'll knock the top off the pain, but drive careful, and don't get too frisky."

There was tension in her voice as she spoke, a tightness around her mouth. She's thinking about the gold too. She leaned in closely and whispered a promise that they had made to each other about a life of wealth and riches as long as they stuck to the agreed plan.

Oh Lord.

He looked at her and thought about the millions of dollars and the possible future they could have together. Stacey figured they had about twenty-four hours before they were free and clear. With a lurch that made him wince, he put the Dodge in gear and lumbered forward.

Chapter 61 - Geist

Standing on a street corner in Rapid City, the man using the name Miller shook his head in wonder. For three days, the wind had blown. Visibility was practically zero. Wind had drifted the snow as high as twelve feet in some sheltered areas, and yet in other areas, it had scraped it clean down to the brown grass or concrete.

And now the sky was a brilliant light blue, the wind was still. Stepping outside the hotel, he had to shield his eyes from the clean white landscape.

He breathed in the crisp air then did it again. *Beautiful*. There was no reason why he would live here, but he could see how it might be attractive. The wildness appealed to him.

He had wasted no time in the hotel room, using the hotel phone and a painfully thin Dansing phone book to go fishing. His first failed visit to Dansing had provided very little except the stolen phone book. This time, he set about using the nosy nature of the locals to his own advantage.

The first phone call was to the radio station.

"K-D-A-N."

"Yeah, this is"—he consulted his Rapid City yellow pages—"K-O-T-A newsroom. Just following up on a wire story about what happened during the blizzard."

"You heard about that?"

Bingo.

"Sure did. What can you tell me?"

"Well, it's Darren White for sure. Least we're pretty sure. The house he was in was blown to smithereens, almost knocked us off the air. The radio tower was on her land—the land of the crazy lady where the blast was. Probably a malfunction in the furnace, that's what I'm guessing—well, it blew her up too. Tossed her out of the house a good fifty feet. Frozen stiff, all of them, by the time we got there. Too damn bad. We were really close—Darren, I mean. He and I used to play football. Not on the same team, but we were both pretty good players, if you know what I mean. I'm Larry Karl."

"Oh! You're Larry Karl?" Geist sounded impressed. He reached for a pad of paper and started taking notes.

"Yeah, back in the glory days. Anyway, Ned Backer is a rancher owns land out by Darren's place. No idea why Darren would go out in weather like that—I mean you couldn't see nothin'. Ned almost ran into the back of his pickup. He was out on his snowmobile, checking the livestock. Stupid enough. I mean when that wind blows, you can get turned around on your own property, but when it's your own livestock, your bread and butter, you take risks, right?"

"So about Darren White."

"Yeah, right. Well, he's the new sheriff, so the talk is that he might have been checking into some peculiar stuff with the new priest, kinda a strange guy, y'know? Anyway, it looks like his truck ran out of gas and he went to get help out at Greta Karns's place—the crazy old gal who lives out by the radio tower, like I said. So we got him and her dead. An accident, probably. And we still can't find the priest. He's probably just getting dug out himself."

"Have you tried calling him?"

"No answer, but that doesn't mean anything necessarily. I mean, it could be he was stuck away from his house and hasn't been able to get home yet."

Geist kept feeding him. "You have a lot of still missing people?"

"Shit, yeah. Our own news gal just came strolling in, la-di-da. Three days, and not a peep from her."

"News gal?"

"Ippy Johnson. She does the news here in the morning. Pain in the ass for me 'cause I've had to cover for her. Showed up at the end of the blizzard, claiming she got stuck and couldn't make it. I'd a got her ass fired, but she's got a thing for me, a little hero worship, y'know? Guess I'm getting soft."

"Anyone else missing?"

"Yeah, a couple of guys that worked at the cemetery, the Catholic cemetery."

"So the new sheriff is dead, and two cemetery employees are missing?"

"Yeah. I thought you knew."

"Yeah, well, about the sheriff I did. Nothing else."

"So you never heard about the old sheriff either, then? Waltraub?" The voice sounded triumphant.

"No... what about him?"

"He's missing too. But not in the storm, at least I don't think so. I saw his truck heading out of town just at the tail end of the storm."

"How do you know it was him?"

"He's got the old '53 Power Ranger that used to be owned by the elevator before it went bankrupt. It's a faded rust color with beat-up black fenders. Not another truck like it. That's why he wasn't around to help with the body or the gold."

The gold. Geist was dumbstruck. The amount of information he had received from phone gossip from a stranger was amazing. He was writing notes frantically.

Geist paused. "Yeah, I heard about the gold but not how much there was."

"Shit! Pardon my French, but shit! Can you imagine finding a bar of gold with a Nazi swastika on it? I mean, Monty Cooper—he's the funeral director—is there, digging around for body parts, rolls over a piece of Darren's coat, and there it is! I bet that crazy lady had it stashed out there. She was a war bride, you know."

Geist tapped his pencil, deciding how to play it. "Yeah, that makes sense. I heard a rumor that there might be more than one bar, though."

"No shit? I never heard that. Who told you that?"

"Didn't get a name. Just a call-in."

"Bet it was Waltraub."

"Why him?"

"Jealous about losing the election, that's why. No

way he coulda won against a local hero like me or Darren, right? So when he lost, then found out about how Darren died trying to track down a gold thief, I bet he called in and tried to smear him."

"You think he had anything to do with the explosion?"

A long pause. "Shit. You think so?"

That was enough for Geist. The best place to start was with the people who were not dead but were missing. *Start with the old sheriff.* "Well, I did hear his name mentioned as a person important to the investigation."

"Wow. I never really liked him much, but I never figured him for a murderer. I just figured that explosion was an accident." Geist wondered how long it might take this new theory to sweep through the town's grapevine.

"This Waltraub. You say he left town?"

"Yep. Saw him myself, heading south toward the interstate after he dropped Ippy off. Hell, he might be heading your way!"

Geist paused. "You say the news woman, Ippy, was dropped off by the sheriff?"

"Yeah. Said she got a ride as she was walking in."

Geist's eyes narrowed. It was too much of a coincidence. *I wonder what she knows?* He patted his attaché case absentmindedly. He knew how to find out.

Chapter 62- Ippy

It had been one day since Stacey had left, and Ippy was nervous. Eight hundred pounds of gold, give or take, was a lot of weight and a lot of money and a whole heck of a lot of temptation.

The gold bar found with Darren White's body was the talk of the town and the talk of the station.

"Got a buddy into commodities." Larry Karl often claimed to have buddies in all walks of life, each with a different claim to inside information and expertise. "Said a bar like that's worth a couple hundred grand minimum."

Larry was holding forth in the lobby. He had a half-hour break for national news and syndication, and a small knot of employees was gathered nearby. Dansing was in the news again. Calls were starting to come in. National media outlets each wanted to know details, some even trying to tie the murders in April in with the gold.

"So anybody see it?" Happy Jack asked.

"The gold or the body?" Ippy was tired of the blatant greed that shone in the eyes of everyone.

Happy Jack tried to look abashed. "Of course, it's terrible about Darren. Great kid. Real tragedy."

Lois brought the topic back. "Ned Backer's wife, Gretchen, said Monty Cooper brought the bar into the house after he found Darren. Cold as sin, she said, and twice as heavy." Lois's eyes shone with the prospect of holding all that sin.

"Coupla hundred grand? That's not that much," Larry scoffed.

"It'll buy *my* house." That got a laugh. Happy Jack's house was worth one tenth that, and everyone knew it.

Ippy excused herself and went to the news booth. Inside, she closed the door and turned on the mic. An open mic meant the "On Air" light outside the booth would turn on, which was the only way to guarantee privacy from the overly attentive Larry Karl.

Shuffling her wire copy, she scanned the latest bulletins for news of Stacey. Or an accident. Or found gold.

Nothing.

She reached for a calculator and punched in some numbers. Five and a half million dollars. She thought about the heft of each bar in her hands and remembered talking about what they would do with the money together.

Then, unwillingly, she thought about what could be done with that money if they didn't have to split it. Her shoulders slumped, and she got a knot in her stomach like the one she'd gotten when she found her husband in bed with another woman.

She smiled, half bitter, half sorrowful. He could be anywhere by now.

She would give him one more day.

Chapter 63 - Geist

The sounds of machines were everywhere outside of the hotel. Men bundled up in coveralls were walking behind what were called snowblowers, machines he had heard of but never seen in use. Elsewhere, larger tractors with buckets, trucks with blades, and skid steer loaders with brooms were attacking the piles of snow. Where the snow wasn't removed, natives plunged through it or over it in winter boots, obviously used to this sort of thing.

A hard-worn taxi with a squeaky alternator belt wheezed to a stop, churning its way through residual snow piled by the curb.

A heavyset man with a ball cap and a gray ponytail heaved up out of the cab and looked at him. "You the one looking for a ride to the airport?"

By way of answering, Miller threw a thumb back to where his pickup stood, snow brushed off and idling. Then he asked his own question. "Is the interstate open?"

"Should be by noon, they say, at least to

Chamberlain."

Miller smiled warmly. "Thanks."

Today was going to be a great day.

Chapter 64- Happy Jack

The man in the chair in Happy Jack's office was from Associated Press. Or UPI. Maybe Reuters? Truth be told, he couldn't remember exactly what the guy had said. He was kind of a bland sort—Anderson, Erickson, or something. He had a card but was so apologetic about it being his last card that Happy Jack never took it. *Like I care.*

"So, uh, this Ippy person. Is that her real name?"

Happy Jack blushed a little. He'd known her name at first, but she always went by Ippy, and when she was not around, everyone called her the Hawaiian hottie, or HH, or names less polite and more descriptive.

He stalled while reaching around for the personnel folders in the file cabinet. "Uh, well, you'll want the exact spelling no doubt... yes. Here it is: Esmeralda Maria Johnson." He spelled it.

"And is she okay? I heard that she was caught in the blizzard."

"Well, not quite. We were worried for a little bit

there. We sent a guy in a snowmobile to get her for work, but she wasn't home. When she did show up, she said she got holed up during the storm. Said she was trying to find the new priest but never did."

"Priest... the one associated with the Catholic cemetery?"

"Yep. She was able to get the scoop on the missing workers. Beat the other media by a full day."

Happy Jack didn't mention that the "other media" consisted of the town newspaper.

"Is she in? I'd like to ask her a few questions."

Happy Jack didn't follow up. He was already losing interest. "Yeah, sure, whatever you need. She's down the hall. Let me know if she can't help you."

The man bent over, picked up a small black attaché case, and gave a vague smile. "I'm sure she will be of great help."

Chapter 65- Ippy

The man walked into the news booth while she was recording. The light was on, and people were supposed to stay out, but some people didn't know the rules. She was already on edge, and the squeak of the door made her jump.

The man seemed apologetic. Average size, nondescript, he was wearing a cheap suit and carrying a small briefcase.

"I'm sorry to disturb you." He turned and latched the door. "I have a few questions."

Ippy had one of her own. *Who the hell are you?*

She opened her mouth but was interrupted by the faint sound of the bell ringing through the soundproofed door.

Ding-ding-ding-ding-ding-ding-ding-ding-ding-ding.

"What's that?" She was instantly alerted. "Was that ten bells?"

Taken aback a little, the man in the suit listened as feet pounded down the hallway. Through the door, Larry

Karl could be heard.

"Ten bells! Shit!"

The door latch twisted from the outside, and Larry shoved his way in, pushing the man in the suit off balance. "Stop recording. We got a ten beller, and it's out of Chamberlain."

Associated Press was the wire service that KDAN subscribed to. Every day, the regularly scheduled allotment of weather, sports, news, and farm markets came chugging down the wire, printed out at sixty words a minute onto an endless spool of cheap yellow paper. If anything unusual happened, they would add that content along with an alarm system that announced its importance.

One bell was scheduled stuff. Three bells signaled maybe a severe storm in the area. Five bells might be used to announce the death of a famous person. Ten bells were rare—an assassination, the announcement of war, something like that. Ten bells seldom happened and signaled everyone in the building to run and see what was up.

Outside, more voices could be heard. Ippy pushed her way past the man with the briefcase to see what was happening. "Holy shit!"

Ippy was taught in broadcast school to never, never, never swear, because the habit might get exposed by accident on air. Larry Karl was apparently not concerned. He swore again. "Holy. Shit."

Ippy looked over his shoulder and read the slug line: Bar of Gold Found.

She ripped the copy out of Karl's hands and read.

The Chaplain of the Chamberlain Salvation Army, Ivan Houser, reports that a bar of gold was dropped off in their drop box sometime in the last day or so. The bar, complete with stamped swastika, was wrapped with a piece of paper saying. "Atonement." Houser says he has contacted Salvation Army headquarters, looking for advice on what to do with the twenty-seven-pound bar...

Ding-ding-ding-ding-ding-ding-ding-ding-ding-ding.

Larry Karl leapt to the teletype for another piece of copy. "They reissued the same story." He ripped it off the teletype and started reading. "No, wait! This one is different. Still in Chamberlain—but Saint Joseph's Indian School:

"The principal at Saint Joseph's Indian School reported this morning that a bar of gold stamped with a Nazi swastika..."

Ding-ding-ding-ding-ding-ding-ding-ding-ding-ding.

Happy Jack got this one.

"This is a different one. From Mitchell. At a Salvation Army drop box there."

Larry Karl asked, "This the same gold that Darren had?"

Lois asked, "Who would do this?"

Happy Jack said, "How many bars of gold are they giving away?"

Ippy felt radiant as she whispered, "All of them."

The man in the suit was not with them. He must have left. No one noticed.

Chapter 66- Geist

It was breakfast in Minneapolis two days out of Dansing, and Geist was looking at the morning paper. By that point, the story had a name, and the headline talked about the atoning angel. In all, thirty-one bars of gold had been dropped off at various charities from South Dakota to Wisconsin, following I-90, until the gold ran out.

Speculation was that all the gold was delivered in less than a day and a half—a short enough time that it caught everyone by surprise. There were no likely candidates.

The paper went on to interview legal experts, who were trying to determine where the gold originated and whose legal property it was. A neighboring column featured the tearful thanks of a soup-kitchen manager who could now look at expanding his mission to hiring a nurse for remedial care.

Geist sighed, tapping his attaché case absentmindedly. *Oh well.*

His thoughts moved from the paper to the next name on the list: a small banker living in Duluth.

*****

She lay in the snow like a broken doll carelessly tossed aside. The entire side of the house was blown away, smoking in the distance. The side of her face was buried in the snow, warm and soft. She blinked away some snowflakes, watching the smoke billow out of her home with surprising detachment.

"Darlin', you all right?" It was Jimmy in his overalls, arms bare to the cold but smooth and muscled the way she remembered them. He was bent over her, blue eyes troubled under furrowed brow.

"Jimmy." She breathed his name in like a breath of summer. She reached up, hand smooth and young again, and brushed the lock of hair back off his forehead.

He bent over and picked her up easily, cradling her in his arms, holding her close. She pressed her face against his chest and breathed in the scent of him— mown hay, sunshine, her Jimmy.

"Girl, you puttin' on some weight?" He hefted her up and closer, rubbing the stubble of his chin against her cheek.

Young and strong again, she laughed and slapped him on the shoulder, her own arm lithe and tan the way it once had been.

"Jimmy." She sighed then said the name again, heart full of joy. "My Jimmy."

"Let's go home."

Epilogue –

Stan Martin

It was spring. Stan and Claire were driving west toward the coast and the setting sun, a baby in the backseat, the window cracked, enjoying the first warm days of spring. The car was back from the repair shop, dents removed, windows repaired, massive engine thrumming contently as they cruised through the central part of Wyoming.

"Getting on empty. Mind if we stop?" Stan and Claire had decided that on this maiden voyage of their family and the newly restored dark-gray car they called the Shark, they would drive randomly, stop where they liked, and listen only to the demands of their whims and the needs of a 440 V8 and a baby.

"There's a camp up here." Claire pointed to the sign.

"Sounds good."

Stan pulled into a gravel parking lot and a cool pine-scented evening next to a rust-colored old Dodge Power

Wagon with "Camp Maintenance" painted on the door.

"Help you?" The woman at the screen door of the building marked "Office" was striking. With a darker complexion and a dimpled smile, she was dressed in a flannel shirt and jeans for the cooler evening. She looked like a model you'd see in camping catalogs, full of health and sunshine.

"Yes, please." Stan's manner was polite. "Do you have a cabin for rent?"

"Yes, we do. My husband's fixing a fence on the trail. He'll be down shortly—oh, he's coming now."

A little bell went off in Stan's memory as he turned to look. Something about the walk. The man had a rolling, almost bearlike gait. The shadows were gone in the gloaming, making it hard to see his face.

The man paused, looking at Stan's car. "That a Chrysler 300?"

"It is."

Taking a few steps forward, Stan could see his face. The man had clear light-blue eyes that looked even lighter in his darkly tanned face. The smile warmed slowly, and teeth glowed in the failing light. "Stan Martin."

Now he recognized him. It was the sheriff from Dansing, Waltraub. The mustache was gone and, with it, about fifteen years. The man seemed younger, lighter.

The woman with the flannel shirt joined them, slipping her arm around the larger man, warm and familiar. "This cowboy able to help you?"

Waltraub looked down at her then nodded to Stan. "I think you may know this fella. This is Stan Martin."

The woman looked at Stan, then at Claire, then at the baby, then smiled. "Pleased to meetcha."

THE END

About the author

JJ Gould has lived throughout the plains states his whole life where he has worked in radio, advertising and funeral service. He and his wife live in Sioux Falls where he is currently working on the sequels to *Dead Air*, *Dead Heat and Dead End.*

40181818R00173

Made in the USA
Lexington, KY
27 May 2019